Praise for William Cobb's past work:

A WALK THROUGH FIRE was nominated for the Pulitzer Prize, the Robert Kennedy Award, the Lillian Smith Award and the Pen-Faulkner Award for fiction. "Because it leaves the reader with no doubt that we truly are all brothers under the skin, A WALK THROUGH FIRE is unquestionably one of the most important and powerful works published this year." said the *West Coast Review of Books*.

Publishers Weekly called HARRY REUNITED "a perceptive black comedy about Southern manners and mores...entertaining and well observed." (July 17, 1995.) HARRY REUNITED was named to its Honor Roll as a notable novel of 1995 by THE YEARBOOK OF THE DICTIONARY OF LITERARY BIOGRAPHY.

Pat Conroy said of SOMEWHERE IN ALL THIS GREEN: "William Cobb writes with uncommon clarity, beauty and mastery of his subject matter." *The Birmingham News* called Cobb "one of the most authentic and distinctive voices in the South." And a review in *Southern Living* said, "SOMEWHERE IN ALL THIS GREEN gives us familiar people in ordinary circumstances, but in Cobb's lyrical hands the results are hauntingly uncommon." This collection stories was named Book of the Year in Fiction by the Alabama Library Association, and Cobb was named Author of the Year for 2000.

"A SPRING OF SOULS raises merry hell with the most familiar conventions of regional melodrama while building a frighteningly credible image of self-righteousness raised to heights of (literal) apocalyptic excess," wrote Bruce Allen in *The Oxford American*. "A darkly compelling novel...powerful and frightening..." said *Library Journal*. From *Southern Living*: "A rare and wonderful thing..." "Vastly entertaining," wrote Peter Landry in *The Philadelphia Inquirer*, as "raw and arresting as the wrath of God. Cobb knows human shortcomings and the feel of pain. His new novel is a fierce book, incisive and insightful." And Wayne Greenhaw, writing in First Draft, said of A SPRING OF SOULS, "It is an anthem to the glory, mystery and madness of the human condition." A SPRING OF SOULS was named a Notable Novel of the Year (1999) by the Dictionary of Literary Biography.

"William Cobb's new novel, WINGS OF MORNING, proves again that he is one of the best novelists practicing the craft in America today," said Pat Conroy. Novelist Sena Jeter Naslund called WINGS OF MORNING "a novel of strange power (that) magnificently recreates the passion, courage and confusion of the Civil Rights struggle." And Lewis Nordan saID, "Long after I finished this book I held these people and their broken hearts in my own mind and heart." "Powerful and compelling" wrote Tom Hull in *Education Digest.* And from *Publishers Weekly*: "Cobb's passionate portrayal of a town on the brink of change does not disappoint." And Elizabeth Doehring, writing in the *Mobile Register*, said, "WINGS OF MORNING tells a riveting story of the American civil rights movement. No writer today has captured it in such an affecting and compelling way from both a historical and a fictional standpoint. Bravo!"

Also by the author:

Pomp amd Circumstance, Lily Trilogy 1
Harry Reunited (novel)
A Walk Through Fire (novel)
The Hermit King and New Stories (novel & stories)
Coming of Age at the Y (novel)
A Spring of Souls (novel)
Wings of Morning (novel)
Somewhere in All This Green (stories)
The Last Queen of the Gypsies (novel)
A Time To Reap (novel)
Captain Billy's Troopers (memoir)
Sweet Home: Stories of Alabama (stories)

A GOOD LIFE

WILLIAM COBB

Livingston Press
The University of West Alabama

Copyright © 2020 William Cobb
All rights reserved, including electronic text
ISBN 13: 978-1-60489-256-7 hardcover
ISBN 13: 978-1-60489-255-0 trade paper
ISBN 13: 978-1-60489-257-4 e-book
Library of Congress Control Number: 2020932310
Printed on acid-free paper
Printed in the United States of America by
Publishers Graphics
Hardcover binding by: HF Group
Typesetting and page layout: Sarah Coffey, Joe Taylor
Proofreading: Barbara Anderson, Jayla Gellington, Erin Watt,
Joe Taylor, Tricia Taylor, Ashley McMinn,
Maddy Owen, Meredith Cobb Smith
Cover layout: Amanda Nolin
Cover photo: Amanda Nolin

Livingston Press is part of The University of West Alabama,
and thereby has non-profit status.
Donations are tax-deductible.
first edition
6 5 4 3 2 1

A GOOD LIFE

CHAPTER ONE

Lily Putnam, Assistant Professor of English at Lakewood College, in her second year of teaching, was assigned to the Yancey Lecture Committee. The Yancey Lectures were held every other year, funded by a generous endowment from Mrs. Willamina Loundes Yancey, Class of '29, who had been married and widowed five times, each time to a wealthier husband, so she was left extremely well off. Mrs. Yancey never attended the lectures, but they were her legacy to the college. The endowment was plush, so the college was able to attract well known, even renowned scholars, from the major universities or even the Ivies.

Lily had been a lowly instructor her first year, and in a move at the end of the academic year that surprised her greatly, she was promoted to Assistant Professor and put on a tenure track.

"There must be some catch," she had said to her friend Brasfield Finch, who was the Writer-in-Residence at Lakewood.

"There is no catch, Lily," he had said, "they are all men. They promoted you because you make their gonads tingle."

"How do you think that makes me feel?" she asked. "I'm a scholar. I don't want to be promoted on my looks."

"Come now, Lily," Finch said, "you can't change the way you look. Oh I suppose you could get yourself up as a bag lady, but that's not your style. Just take advantage of what the Creator, should there be such a thing, gave you. You know you are beautiful and sexy."

"But that's not all I am," she said, pouting.

"No, and anybody with any sense—that, of course does not extend to the administration of this institution—knows that. So quit worrying about it and enjoy being a professor."

"*Assistant* Professor," she said.

Brasfield Finch was also a member of the Yancey Lecture Committee. He dressed in what Willow Behn, another senior member of the department—and a mentor of Lily's—called his "uniform": scuffed boots, faded jeans, a denim work shirt and a worn corduroy vest. He sported a beard that was famous in academic circles all over the state of Florida. It was overgrown and bushy, so long that it hung down to his belly, and he tied the end in a point with a piece of colorful string. His thinning hair hung down in ringlets to his shoulders. Finch had published a couple of moderately successful novels early in his career; they didn't sell well but they garnered some positive reviews in *Publishers' Weekly* and *Kirkus*. Since then he had published a few short stories, all in small journals. He had been working on a new novel for years; Lily had read two chapters of it and thought it his very best work.

"I think this year we should invite someone in Kinesiology," Lillian Lallo, who was co-chairperson of the Yancey Committee, said. They were meeting in the seminar room on third floor Comer.

Brasfield Finch snorted. "A glorified P. E. teacher?" he asked. "I think not."

"Well then, someone from the business world," Lillian, who was a member of the business department, said.

"We are not a corporation, Lillian," Finch said, "we are an institution of higher learning. We do not need the greedy tarnish of the corporate world."

"Mr. Finch," Lillian said, "you are a very difficult man."

"So I've been told," he said.

Lily looked on this exchange with amusement. She adored the older man, so much so that she had had a fling with him the previous year. He had a lot of gray in his hair and beard, but he was still more than potent in his sexual apparatus, which had pleased Lily immensely. He had broken off their fling himself.

"You need a younger man, Lily, not an old fart like me," he'd said.

"But..." she had protested.

"Listen to me, Lily," he'd said, "trust me."

"But there's really no one," she'd said.

Lily had looked over the group of new hires this fall. One man, new in the physics department, seemed promising; she had gone out with him shortly before classes had started. He had made no move toward her at all and had smoothly rebuffed any moves she made. She wondered if her gaydar had let her down. The rest of the men were either married or seemed soft and wimpy, not to her taste at all. There was one attractive woman, new in the history department, who set off strong vibes in Lily's bisexual gaydar. Lily had flirted with her at the new faculty reception at Flower Hill, the president's residence on campus, but had not gotten much response. Lily suspected that Paulette Jefferson, the dean's butch wife—who also taught in history—had already gotten to her.

"I think," Finch said, "with the amount of the stipend, we could get a first rate scholar from Yale or Harvard. Or we could get a writer of renown."

Now it was Lillian Lallo's time to snort. "*Really Mr. Finch*," she said, obviously remembering and referring to the disaster of the previous spring, when the college had invited Lenora Hart, one of America's most beloved writers, author of the classic *To Lynch a Wild Duck*, and she had made a drunken spectacle of herself. So much so that the episode, when Hart was the speaker at the annual Senior Day convocation, had put the president of the college, John W. Stegall, III, in the hospital suffering from high anxiety and tension; he had insisted that he was having a heart attack, but that had been a false alarm. "Surely you don't want to have another *writer*!" Lallo went on.

"Why not?" Finch asked. "I warned John—I warned everybody—about Hart. Nobody would listen to me. Not every writer is like that."

"I have had recommended to me this writer Pat Conroy and this poet, James Dickey," Shari Bulgarski from the music department put in. "But I understand that they both drink and are of dubious morals."

"Dickey is a poet. I was talking about a real writer," Finch said, "a writer of fiction, like Conroy."

"And like *you* I suppose," Bulgarski said sarcastically.

"Yes. And like Charles Dickens and William Faulkner. At any rate, I know both those gentlemen, Conroy and Dickey—unfortunately I was born too late to know Chuck and Bill—and you are right. Like most penman, they partake of the corn. The last time the three of us were together we drank three quarts of Wild Turkey and ate several bottles of green olives stuffed with anchovies. We shucked and ate four big bags of raw oysters, into the night. It was a fun—and extremely literary—evening."

"Ugh!" Bulgarski said.

"Mr. Finch," Lillian Lallo said, "I am interested in neither your choice of food and beverages nor your drunken friends. Thank you."

"You're welcome," said Finch.

"And Toni Morrison," Lily interjected. "She's a fiction writer!" It was the first thing she had said in the meeting. Morrison was the subject of Lily's uncompleted dissertation.

"Yes! Perhaps we could invite Ms Morrison," Finch said enthusiastically.

"Oh, that would be peachy great!" Lily said.

"*Peachy great*?! Really, Lily," Lallo said.

"Hey, that rhymes," Finch said. "*You're* the poet, Lillian."

"Like a cold day in hell I am," Lillian said.

"There is no reason for vulgarity," Shari Bulgarski said.

"What?" Lillian asked.

"Hell," Bulgarski said.

Lillian snorted. "Stuff it, Shari," she said.

Finch watched the two women spar. You never knew when you could pick up a character for whatever fiction you were working on. Shari was a big woman who taught voice, a soprano, and she dressed sloppily. It was hard to tell if whatever she had on was a shawl or a cape or something else entirely. Black slacks protruded over her heavy shoes, and her brownish hair was a loose rat's nest on her head that showed no sign of recent brushing. Lillian was a small, thin boned woman with dim, sallow red hair done in tight ringlets. She wore a suit that looked a size too large for her. Her mouth was narrow lipped and pinched.

"At any rate," Finch said, "Mrs. Yancey specified in her bequest that we invite a scholar. And as much as I abhor scholars, I have a suggestion." Finch shoved a stack of papers across the table. "I propose," he said, "that we invite Dr. Charles Stewart, an eminent Yeats scholar at Harvard. Here are his credentials, his books and publications."

Lily sighed. "Not Toni Morrison?"

Finch put his hand on top of hers and smiled. "Perhaps we can get Toni on the Concert and Lecture series."

"You abhor 'scholars?'" Lallo said. "Then what are you doing on a college faculty?"

"Lillian, you don't know how many times I've asked myself the same question. Anyway, I met Dr. Stewart once, at an MLA meeting in New York. We had a drink together."

"Just *one*?" Lillian Lallo spat.

"Well, actually, two or three, I don't remember. But he is a personable, *young* man, very attractive..." And here he squeezed Lily's hand, a gesture not lost on either of the other women. "...and he would be wonderful with our students. He would make the perfect Yancey Lecturer."

"Huh," Shari grunted.

"Let's hear *your* proposal, then, Miss Bulgarski," Finch said.

"Listen, Buster, *I'm* running this meeting!" Lillian said.

"I don't have a proposal," Bulgarski said.

"You need to address your proposal to *me*," Lillian said to her.

"I said I don't have one."

"Well, then, Lillian? Let's hear yours," Finch said.

"Are you the chair, Mr. Finch?" Lillian asked through tight lips.

"No, and you're not either, Lillian. Wallace Jefferson is chairman of this committee, and he's not here."

"I am co-chair!"

"Do you have a proposal? If not, what do you think of Dr. Stewart?"

She leafed through the papers. "I suppose he's all right," she said in a hard, raw tone. Finch knew he had buffaloed her, trounced her. He smiled warmly.

Just then the door to the seminar room opened and there stood the bulk of Dean Wallace Jefferson in his XXXXL blue serge suit. He bustled into the room and wedged himself into a chair. Jefferson crowded a room just by entering it. Dean Jefferson was still a professor of history, and he represented that department on the committee. Most of their proposals over the years were of men so obscure of reputation that they were usually voted down as inappropriate for a Yancey Lecturer. They had been agitating for years for their own lecture series, since traditionally the English Department had been the most influential voice on the Yancey committee, but they had not yet found a wealthy donor to fund it. Mrs. Willamina Loundes Yancey's major had been Home Economics, a department that had shrunk and had finally been merged into the Social Sciences (History, Political Science and Social Work) and had disappeared, for all practical purposes.

"Sorry I'm late," the dean said, "I had a meeting."

Finch said: "Administrators have more meetings than the Pope has beads."

Jefferson cut his eyes at Finch. "I see you are in fine form this afternoon, Brasfield," he said.

"Yes," Finch said, "I am. We were just concluding the meeting, actually. We have settled on Dr. Charles Stewart, a Yeats scholar from Harvard."

"Let *me* tell him," Lallo said.

"Okay, Lillian, you tell him."

"Dr. Stewart is one of the most admired scholars in America. He is an expert on W. B. Yeats," she said.

"Now, who is that?" Jefferson said.

"Dr. Stewart? Or W. B. Yeats?" Lillian asked.

"This Yeats person," Jefferson said. "Isn't he a poet?"

"Yes. *Was*. He is deceased," Finch said. "He is one of the greatest poets of Ireland."

"Ireland?" Jefferson said. "What's wrong with America?"

"Dr. Stewart is an *American* scholar, Wallace. That should satisfy your nationalistic tendencies just fine," Finch said.

"But why not Robert Frost?" Jefferson asked.

"Pardon?"

"Why don't we get an expert on Frost? You know, 'Good fences make good neighbors' and so forth."

"I don't think you quite grasp the meaning of that poem, Wallace," Finch said, "but never mind."

Lily laughed out loud.

"Now what is so funny, Miss Putnam?" the Dean said.

"Nothing," Lily said, "I...I was just thinking of something I dreamed last night."

"A wet dream probably," muttered Shari Bulgarski under her breath.

Lily ignored her. She knew that most of the other women on campus did not like her because of her looks. They assumed she was dumb because of her figure and blonde hair, which she wore in a short, almost mannish style. Her legs were long and shapely, and she accentuated them with micro miniskirts, the more micro the better. She had learned to handle other women; she had had lots of practice. And she knew that Brasfield Finch and Willow Behn, an older woman friend in the department, considered her very intelligent, which she was. She suspected even Wallace Jefferson, with whom she had

had some awkward moments during the previous year, knew it as well.

"Well," Jefferson said, sighing contentedly, "it seems that my committee has done a lot of good work today. I congratulate you."

"Thank you, boss," Finch said. Jefferson glared at him.

"I suppose this Yeats business is your work, Brasfield," he said.

"Not at all," Finch said. "Lillian?"

"It was a committee decision, Dean Jefferson," Lallo said. "We feel that this Stewart will be perfect for our students. He is young, attractive…" And here she glanced at Lily. "…and very well respected in the academic community. If he accepts, we can't go wrong."

"Don't be too overconfident, Lillian," the dean said. "Remember that awful playwright who seduced all the boys in the theater department; he came very highly recommended. And then last year, with Brasfield's friend Lenora Hart…"

"Don't blame it on me," Finch said, "I warned you and John about her, and you didn't listen to me."

"No, I must admit we didn't," Jefferson said. "But that's water under the proverbial bridge. I just hope this Stewart fellow isn't one of your drinking buddies, Brasfield."

"He is," Shari Bulgarski interjected.

"I said we had a couple of drinks together at MLA in New York once. He is hardly my 'buddy.'"

"But he drinks," the dean said.

"*You* drink, Wallace," Finch said.

"But not like you. Snorting all day. Going to class drunk."

"I've never been to class drunk in my life," Finch said.

"They can smell it on you. I've heard it for years."

"Smell does not equate to 'drunk,' Wallace," Finch said, "and you know it. I teach better with a bit of Scotch under my belt. So what?"

"If you didn't have tenure, you'd be long gone, Mr. Finch," the dean said. "Somehow there are still some members of the board of trust who are impressed with your little…literary efforts."

"I have it on pretty good authority that I'm not the only one who drinks on campus during the day," Finch said.

The dean looked briefly at Lily then away. "Yes, well..." he said. "Is there anything else we need to discuss? Get me this Stewart's address and we'll officially invite him."

"Done," Finch said. "I declare this meeting adjourned."

"Hey!" said Lillian Lallo.

CHAPTER TWO

Willow Behn sat at her desk, having just gotten off the phone with Eloise Hoyle, the president's secretary. It still annoyed her that John Stegall had his secretary call her to arrange a friendly tennis match. Even when John was rising through the ranks of the music department (his specialty was the saxophone) he had had the departmental secretary call Willow; it continued when he was chair of music, then dean, and now president. Willow had been a youngish assistant professor, single, when she had gotten the first call, and it puzzled her why Stegall had settled on her as a tennis partner. He was married, of course, and Willow was under no illusion that she was more than an acceptably attractive, taller, somewhat older woman. Taller by a head than John Stegall, who had showed up on the courts dressed in new tennis whites from head to toe, and she had trounced him badly. Over the years he had never beaten her, but he still had his secretary call to make a tennis date. Willow, observing him as president and on the court, had deduced that he had a strong masochistic streak.

Willow Behn was now a full professor, and many people on campus, including Brasfield Finch and Lily Putnam, considered her to be far and away the most laudable scholar among the entire faculty. Years ago she had run the gamut of the white-haired old men in the English department at Vanderbilt—the good old boys, many left over from the Fugitive years—to become one of the first women to gain a PhD from there, even though they all had considered her uppity and constantly put obstacles in her path. She *forced* them to respect her. She never made below an A+ in any course; they didn't know quite what to do with her. In seminars she met their sarcasm with her own, which seemed to frazzle them. When it came time for her dissertation, she wrote an annotated edition of Byron's letters to Keats, with an appendix 179 pages long, which she worked on for an entire year in London, at the Victoria and Albert Museum, which housed the Byron letters. Her committee all had to agree that the text was brilliant. They had no choice but to grant her the degree, with honors.

With no support from the faculty, except for one senile old Romantics professor, she submitted the book to Yale University Press, which published it to glowing notices from all over the country. For a few years she was quite well known as a dazzling new Byron scholar, much in demand at MLA and other conferences. But Willow had not followed up with another book; she had been working on a book on Georges Sand for years, and she occasionally gave a paper at the South Atlantic Modern Language Association, and that was enough for her. Some of her colleagues in other universities questioned why she stayed at little Lakewood College. "Because I like it," was her answer, "I am happy here. You should try a small liberal arts college," she would say to them, "it'll make you live longer."

John Stegall showed up on this beautiful September afternoon with a crisp new set of tennis whites, which Willow suspected his wife had selected for him. (She imagined that Nelle chose all his clothing, "outfitted" him.) His new shoes blindingly reflected the sunlight, as did his polo shirt and his baggy shorts. He wore a "cute" wrinkled-brim white hat.

They lagged for serve, and Willow won. Her first serve was like a shot over the net and spun John's racket around. "Fifteen, love," she said. Why hadn't she gotten totally bored with this? Time after time, the same. She supposed she must have sadistic tendencies herself. Her second serve was an ace that went by him before he even moved his racket. He was grinning as though he had won the point. "Thirty, love," she said. "Are you ready, John?"

"Bring it on!" he said, bouncing around.

"Maybe you should back up a little," she said.

"Don't tell me how to play tennis, Willow," he said. "I've been playing since you were a little girl!"

He seemed completely divorced from reality.

He managed to return her next serve (she let up a little bit) high over the net. It bounced higher than her head and she softly returned it, hoping at least to get a rally started. He crushed the ball directly into the net. "forty-five, love," she said. "Game point."

Then it was game. She then pinged him the balls, which he struggled with. His hands didn't seem to be large enough to hold two balls at once, so he kept the second ball at his feet. His first serve went directly into the net. His second serve was a good one, and Willow approached the bounce and slammed it into the corner, right by his ear. "Love, fifteen," she said. And so it went.

Brasfield Finch, sitting in his office with the door open, watched Lily Putnam walk down the hall to her office, her hips undulating under the short skirt, her legs long and smooth and tan. She was the most delectable piece of woman flesh the faculty at Lakewood had seen in decades, and Finch had worked long and hard to get the department to hire her. The two older women in the department, scholarly spinsters, in addition to Willow Behn, all of whom Finch referred to as the "nuns," did not want to hire her at all. They wanted a tweedy little pipe smoking wimp from Ole Miss, a new doctorate, and Lily was ABD (all but dissertation), and even though Lily claimed otherwise, Finch knew that she had done very little work on it the previous year. He had held out for her, because he knew Lily would improve the decor of Comer Hall immensely, as far as he was concerned. He was sympathetic with the girl about her lack of progress, because they loaded her down with composition courses, and a young woman like her had to have some social life, to which he had contributed in some small degree with occasional drinks at Stache's and a brief fling in his king sized bed, for which

Lily Putnam was absolutely as true as advertised. She did not need to waste her time and energy in scholarly pursuits; leave that to the "nuns."

Finch was not a scholar; he was a writer and a teacher of writing. He held an MFA from the University of Southern Mississippi, because the administration at the time considered that a terminal degree for him. Not so the new regime. Wallace Jefferson had said, "A Master's degree is a Master's degree, Finch. As long as I am dean, no one will become a full professor without a doctorate." So Brasfield Finch was an Associate Professor, which really suited him just fine as long as no one messed around with his classes or interfered with his habit of nipping on his Scotch all day. Professors made only pennies more than Associates, and Finch did not care that much about money at all.

Finch was quite fond of Lily, and of Willow Behn as well, though he didn't think Willow cared that much for him. She did not suffer his drinking, as if it was any of her goddamn business. His reputation on campus was that of a profligate drinker, but he knew he was an excellent teacher and his students—certain ones of them, that is—adored him and respected him. He did not care about the others.

Finch figured Charles Stewart to be a promising prospect for Lily's bed for the week he would be on campus. He had liked the young man immensely; they had actually had four of five drinks, Finch couldn't really remember how many, and had ended the evening singing college fight songs with Sonny, the blind black pianist in the Blue Bar of the Algonquin Hotel. Charlie Stewart was a convivial lush, which fully suited Finch's qualifications for a Yancey Lecturer, in addition, of course, to his reputation as a Yeats scholar, which seemed to Brasfield a considerably lesser priority. In fact, literary critics were not his favorite people, but they seemed to go with the territory. If you were going to be a writer, there would always be critics, poised to blast you or praise you, more often the former. Finch hated reviewers, most of them anyway, with a passion; he only respected those who had the good sense to give him a good notice. All the others must have had hangovers or had fights with their wives the previous night, because Finch knew in his heart that his novels were not as bad as some of them said they were. But he didn't lose any sleep over them; to hell with them.

He made a mental note to have Eloise Hoyle lay in a supply of good Scotch in the guest quarters in Hill House, where all the visiting scholars and writers and musicians stayed (except, of course, for Lenora Hart, who had insisted on a five star hotel in Tallahassee). Eventually, he supposed, there would be a historian there, provided the history department ever got their shit together. Finch smiled to himself, thinking of the ineffectual Wallace Jefferson and his butch wife Paulette. Then he closed his eyes and recalled the vision of Lily walking down the hall. Ahhh, there is still real beauty in the world!

Finch leaned over and opened his filing cabinet and pulled out a bottle of Chivas Regal and poured himself a hefty drink into a Lakewood College mug that he kept on his desk. It was his preparation for his writing workshop. Finch himself read only those manuscripts from his good, serious students; the others he had them read aloud in class and commented on them off the top of his head. This afternoon he had scheduled two stories by two sorority girls who had somehow blundered into his class, probably thinking it would be a crip. The first one was entitled "Untitled," which made Finch groan and turn it face down on his desk. The second was entitled "Make Me," by a fetching little brunette who openly flirted with Finch; he was certain that the title did not mean what he thought it meant—which would probably have made it a more interesting story—because even though the girl was a flirt, he could tell there was nothing there. She was a Southern Baptist from some country town in the Panhandle. Finch was not above sampling the wares of his students; in fact he had had some exceptionally satisfying trysts with some of them, even Southern Baptists, as a matter of fact. Some of them seemed driven, as though he had set them free.

A Good Life

Others not so much. But he had to be careful.

The first girl to read, the author of the "untitled" piece, was named Lucy Pennypacker, from Moss Point, Mississippi. (Finch knew where they were from; at the beginning of each workshop he had them fill out 3x5 index cards with their names, class, dorms, and home towns and—just in case—their phone numbers.) Her story was about an elderly man who goes fishing in a lake. He fishes and he fishes and he catches nothing. It went on and on in that vein, written in short, child-like sentences, and Miss Pennypacker read it in a dull monotone. The old man fished and he caught nothing and that was it. When she was finished, Finch asked,

"And?"

"And what?" Miss Pennypacker asked.

"Nothing happens in this piece, Miss Pennypacker," he said.

"He *fishes*, Mr. Finch," she said.

"Yes, but there is no conflict."

"Oh, that comes later," she said. She was tall and thin, as tall as her sorority sister, Angie Dearbon, was short and squatty. They were like Mutt and Jeff.

"Later?" Finch asked.

"Yes. This is the first chapter of a novel. About my grandfather. The conflict comes later."

"A novel? How much of this *novel* have you written?"

"Oh just this much," she said.

"And have you planned your novel? Outlined it? Made notes?"

"No. I'm just letting it come. I'll find out what the conflict is when I get there."

It was an answer that Finch might well have given to a similar question about his own work, but it infuriated him to hear it coming from this sorority girl, who knew as little about writing novels as he knew about pledge classes and such.

"Well, I'm afraid your reader—if by any chance you might

ever have one—will not make it past your opening chapter, Miss Pennypacker," he said. "There is nothing to draw your reader in. There is no drama. What do you think, Mr. Pendarvis?" Jack Pendarvis was one of the two truly talented and serious writers in the workshop, the other being his friend Tommy Franklin. Jack was a highly innovative young writer. He was more of the Barth-Italo Calvino school, whereas Tommy was a psychological realist.

"Well, it was okay, I guess," Jack said. He had a tendency to be too nice to the other students.

"Okay? Well, *that's* very perceptive." He peered at the girl. "Your style. Have you been reading Hemingway, Miss Pennypacker?"

"Who?"

"Ernest Hemingway. Never mind." Finch sighed. "Does anybody else have a comment?"

"Well," Miss Dearbon said, "I liked the character of her grandfather."

"Her grandfather?" Finch said. "This is a memoir? I thought it was a novel."

"It *is* a novel," Miss Pennypacker said.

"I mean the character based on her grandfather," Angie said.

"Then it is *fiction*. It is not her grandfather. Get that straight. There is a vast difference between memoir and fiction. Maybe it would be better if Miss Pennypacker wrote it as a memoir, then she could get away, perhaps, with an opening chapter in which absolutely nothing happens but an old coot fishing, to—incidentally—absolutely no avail."

"Don't call my grandfather an 'old coot!'" Lucy said.

Finch sighed again. "He is either your grandfather, or *not* your grandfather, Miss Pennypacker, make up your mind. What do you think of this opening chapter, Mr. Franklin?"

"Well," Franklin drawled, "I sort of agree with you, Mr. Finch. There is no grabber." Franklin had the kind of rugged good looks that drove women crazy. He wore a short little ponytail on the back of his head. Finch rarely saw Tommy around campus when he didn't have a winsome coed on his arm. Both girls perked up at his comment.

"What do you mean, 'grabber?'" Lucy asked. She smiled for the first time in the workshop.

"Like Mr. Finch said, there is nothing to draw the reader in," Franklin said. "Maybe he could fall out of the boat and someone on the shore could jump in and save him. And he could bond with whoever it was. Maybe even a little girl. Then you have a grabber that will pull your reader on to the next chapter."

"But he didn't fall out of the boat!" Lucy said.

"If it's fiction, he *could*," Tommy said.

"Now we're getting somewhere," Finch said. "Now you have a novel, Miss Pennypacker. Listen to what Tommy says."

"He didn't fall out of the boat," Lucy said defiantly.

"I give up, then," Finch said. "Miss Dearbon? Your story entitled 'Make Me.'" Franklin and Pendarvis both chuckled. Finch knew they read the title exactly as he did.

Angie Dearbon read her story dramatically, with voice inflections and hand gestures. It was about a beautiful girl—short of stature, of course—from St. Louis, who gets lost while driving across the river in western Kentucky and gets rescued by a handsome young man driving a black Miata.

"Now *that* could be the start of a novel," Finch said when she was finished. "Maybe a romance novel, which is what you probably should be writing anyway, if you must insist on writing anything at all."

"It's a short story, I don't want to write a novel," Angie said.

"As you wish," Finch said. "By the way, Miss Dearbon, what is the significance of your title? Did something interesting happen in the back seat of her Chevrolet? Or is the back seat of that model Chevrolet even large enough to accommodate—as they say on *The Dating Game*—'making whoopee?'"

The girl looked puzzled. She didn't have any idea what he was talking about. She probably had *some* inkling, but her little mind would not let the notion form. "It's called 'Make Me' because she is from Missouri," she said.

"Pardon?"

"Missouri is the 'make me' state."

Finch stared at her. After a minute he said, "If I am not seriously mistaken, Miss Dearbon, Missouri is the 'show me' state, not the 'make me' state."

"Oh," she said, "then I'll change the title."

Finch sighed for the final time in that day's workshop. "Class dismissed," he said.

He hastened to his office and poured himself a quick snort of Scotch. He was suddenly aware of a presence in his open doorway; turning, he saw Lucy Pennypacker standing there. She was so tall that her blonde hair almost touched the top of the door frame. She wore a long, India print skirt down to her ankles.

"Nice skirt, Miss Pennypacker," Finch said, "what can I do for you?"

"Thanks," she said. "I can smell your liquor all the way over here."

"Oh, I'm sorry," he said, "would you care for a drink?"

"No, I most certainly would not," she said. "I don't drink."

"To each his own," Finch said. He smiled. "Or *her* own, whatever." She just stood there. "Did you wish to speak with me about something?"

"I don't like the way you belittled me in class today," she said.

Finch leaned back in his office chair and it squeaked under him. He peered at her. "First," he said, "I must congratulate you on the use of the word 'belittled.' I wouldn't think it'd be common usage in Moss Point, Mississippi."

"There you go," she said.

"And second," Finch continued, "I—we—did not 'belittle' you. We were simply discussing your story, or chapter. It's called *workshopping*, Miss Pennypacker. That's what writers, especially apprentice writers, do. So that we can learn from our readers. And our critics." Finch cringed inwardly at the word *critic.*

"I didn't think you gave me much to 'learn,' Mr. Finch."

"I thought I was very succinct in my response to your chapter, Miss Pennypacker. You should listen to me and Mr. Franklin. If you would take into consideration our observations, I think you could learn a great, great deal about fiction writing."

"I don't want anybody else telling me how to write my novel," she said.

"Then why, if I may ask, are you taking this class? You can get praise if you read it to your Aunt Hattie, if that's what you want."

"I don't have an Aunt Hattie."

"I meant Aunt whoever. Or your mother."

"My mother's deceased."

"Your father, then."

"He is, too."

"I'm very sorry for your loss, dear, but surely you have some-one you could read it to. What about Angie Dearbon?"

"She's too busy with boys right now. *My* boyfriend, as a mat-ter of fact," she said.

"Oh, I'm sorry to hear that, too, but I can't get into such as that. Girl stuff. I have neither the time nor the energy." She didn't seem to have anything else to say. "I'll tell you what, Miss Pen-nypacker," he said after a minute, "why don't you rewrite your chapter, considering the comments in class. Turn it in to me in two weeks, and we'll go from there."

"Re*write* it?" she said. "You mean write it again?"

"Yes. Revise it. What you have, really, is a first draft. Revise. That's what writers do. Many writers feel that it is only in revision that the true nature of the piece on which they're working takes form. Give that a try, why don't you?"

"I don't want to rewrite the whole thing," she said.

Finch leaned back and gazed levelly at the girl. He looked at her for a full minute. "As you wish, Miss Pennypacker, as you wish," he finally said. "After all, it's your novel, your chapter. If you are satisfied with it, who am I to tell you otherwise? Go and do what you want with it! Let it fly! Write like the wind! I wish you all the good luck and good fortune in the world. Maybe it'll be a best seller. I truly hope it will be." She was looking at him with her eyes narrowed and her lips pinched, as though she was certain he was still "belittling" her. "I *mean* it. Go," he said. "Get busy."

CHAPTER THREE

Lily was anxious and excited about Charles Stewart coming to campus. Brass (which is what she called Brasfield Finch) had told her as much as he knew about him.

"He's *fine*, Lily," Brass had said, "you'll keep him busy."

She had looked him up in the Harvard Catalogue in the library. They actually had pictures of the faculty in their catalogue, though they were postage stamp in size. Still, she could tell that Dr. Stewart was a specimen. He looked younger than his thirty nine years.

"He's not a wimp," Finch told her, "not like our own dear Rufus." He was referring to their department chair, Rufus Doublet (who pronounced his name Doo-blay), who was, as Lily knew from experience, a closet homosexual even though he himself might not have fully known it yet.

Lily had been re-reading Yeats' poetry in anticipation of the scholar's visit, even though it would not occur until the spring semester. She had always liked Yeats, though she had never had a course in him. She *had* taken a course in graduate school in The English Lyric, which began with Medieval street ballads and came down to the poetry of Yeats, though by the end of the semester they had had little time for him. The professor, an elderly gentleman nearing retirement, brought his guitar to class and sang many of the lyrics. Lily remembered, and had especially liked, "The Song of Wandering Aengus" and "The Lake Isle of Innisfree." In her own reading, she liked "The Crazy Jane" poems. She was particularly fond of the lines: "Love has pitched its tent / In the place of excrement." Not the most lyrical of Yeats' lines, but Lily thought he had really nailed it. She knew Yeats was not being a nasty old man, but was talking about the power of love to endure and prevail among the most smelly and unpleasant aspects of human life. Not that Lily's place of excrement was unpleasantly smelly; she had been told once by an older woman with whom she had had an affair in graduate school that she smelled and tasted like a "lavender oyster." And she had never had any complaints from any of the myriad men and women with whom she'd been intimate since. Brasfield Finch, the most recent person to rim her, told her she tasted like "brown sugar."

"Then why don't you come back for more?" she had asked him.

"I may yet," he'd answered. "But first I want you to sample Stewart. I think he's just what you need."

"His bio says he's a Mormon," Lilly said.

"Mormons don't have peckers?" Finch said.

"I just mean that…well…maybe he's a religious guy."

"A Yeats scholar? From Harvard? Likely not."

"You never know," she said.

"Come on, Lily. I think you're just preparing yourself for a letdown. Quit thinking about it. It'll happen, believe me. He'll take one look at you and…blam!"

"Okay," she said. After all, she had several months to think about it.

Lily was sitting in her office having a conference with one of her sophomore students, an extremely good looking boy named Sydney Polemus. Sydney was not any taller than she was (5'6") and he was stocky and thickly built. He was also a brilliant student. He had written a paper for Lily entitled "When 'Or' Becomes 'And': A Movement Toward the Phoenix Metaphor in *Samson Agonistes*." At first she had been certain he had plagiarized it; she had searched in various indexes and Milton studies in the library, to no avail. He had read the long poem on his own (it was not in the sophomore anthology of World Literature; there were only excerpts from *Paradise Lost*.) His first short paper had been an A, but nothing like this.

"Mr. Polemus, this is a superior paper, worthy of a senior English major or even a graduate student," Lily said.

"Thanks," he said. "Do I get an A+?"

"It is certainly an A+ paper, especially for a sophomore survey course. Are you an English major?"

"I haven't decided yet."

"You should consider majoring in English. Who is your advisor?"

"Miz Stern, in the art department." Laurie Stern was a new instructor. The senior faculty had a habit of loading down fresh instructors with advisees, so they wouldn't have to bother with too many of them.

"Perhaps I should speak with her," Lily said, "would you like me to do that?"

"I guess," he said. "About what?"

"Maybe majoring in English?" she asked.

He shrugged, and remained silent. He didn't seem very enthusiastic about declaring his major as English, or anything else. As Lily looked at him she saw him gaze at her legs. He focused on where her mini skirt hugged her upper thighs, as though he were itching to lean down and get a better look.

"Mr. Polemus," she said, and he looked up and blushed, "I'm still a little troubled about this paper. Are you sure you didn't have some help with it?"

"Well," he said, "I didn't copy it."

"But you had some help with it?"

"I wrote it myself, but my Aunt Julia helped me some."

"Your Aunt Julia? Is she an English teacher?"

"Yes mam. At Indian Springs School in Alabama. I'm from Birmingham and when I went home me and her talked about it."

"She and I," she said.

"Mam?"

Being from Alabama, and having gone as an undergraduate to Birmingham-Southern College, Lily certainly knew of Indian Springs. It was one of the best prep schools in the southeast.

"So she teaches at Indian Springs?" Lily asked.

"Yes mam. She got her Master's Degree at Bread Loaf School of English in Vermont. Have you ever heard of Bread Loaf?"

"Of course."

"Anyway, she had this course in Milton taught by this little guy from Columbia University. She said he was the smartest man she'd ever known, and the best teacher. I forget his name."

Edward Taylor, I would bet, thought Lily. He had come as a visiting scholar to Emory when she was there. He was truly a gifted and accomplished scholar, and his reputation as a teacher of Milton was legend.

"So she helped you with your paper?" Lily asked. "How much?"

"Well…" He hesitated. "See, she wrote this paper with the same title as mine for this little guy (Lily smiled at the description of Ted Taylor as a "little guy") and she let me read hers."

"So how much of her paper did you use?"

"Well…just sort of…the general outline," he said. He shifted in the chair. He looked away from her. Then back. His eyes lingered on her breasts for a moment before he met her eyes. He couldn't help himself.

"Just the 'general outline?' What do you mean?" she asked.

"Just…you know…she *explained* the paper to me. Sort of point by point."

"Point by point?"

"You know," he said.

"No, Mr. Polemus, I don't know. How much of this paper is hers and how much is yours?" He didn't answer. "Sydney…may I call you Sydney?" He nodded. "Sydney, I must tell you that this paper is far, far more sophisticated than the work I usually get in this class. It is way, way better than your first paper, even though that one was an A."

There was a long pause. The air in her office was heavy. He was staring at her legs. Then he looked up at her again.

"Am I in trouble?" he asked. Before she could frame an answer he said, "Because I'm Freddy the Falcon this year, and I would die if I had to give that up. Or get kicked out of school, or something."

"Freddy the Falcon?"

He had tears in his eyes now. "The school mascot," he said, "you know, at the basketball games. And sometimes around campus, at big events."

"Yes," she said, "I've seen you."

"You must have seen Lindsey Pruett. She was Freddy all last year. It's a big deal, Miss Putnam, we're elected by the student body and all. It's a great honor."

"Well," she said, "I certainly wouldn't want to interfere with that."

"You mean…I'm not in trouble?"

She looked him over. His chest was thick and bulky, and his jeans were tight on his legs, which were good—youthful, of course—legs. He had a sizable bulge at his crotch.

"No, you're not in trouble. Right now, Sydney, this is just between the two of us. We don't need to involve anyone else, the honor council or anyone. Deal?"

"Well…yeah."

"Do you have a girlfriend, Sydney?" she asked.

He looked puzzled. "Well…no. I date some I mean, like that. But I don't have a steady girlfriend, no."

"Good," she said. "Here's the deal, my man, you admit to me that you handed in your aunt's paper, then I allow you to do the second paper again. And I will help you with it one night in my apartment. That's the best I can offer."

His eyes widened. She gave him her most seductive stare. He looked her up and down. Blushing, he actually licked his lips.

"Your…apartment?" he stammered.

"Yes," she said, "Sydney."

"Okay," he said. "I admit it!"

"Let me ask you, Sydney, did you even read *Samson Agonistes*?"

"No mam," he said. He grinned with a new self-confidence. *He is already a **man**,* Lily thought, *unfortunately.*

When he was gone, Lily sat looking out the window. Her office looked out over the east end of the quad, and she could see across to the library. She was thinking about last year, her only tryst with a student; he had been a stud third baseman on the baseball team who was in her sophomore survey. It had been an extremely satisfying encounter, though he was a bit inexperienced and somewhat clumsy. But he had had a steady girlfriend, and it dawned on Lily that the last thing she needed was an angry, jealous coed coming down on her. And she also suspected that he probably bragged to his buddies on the team, and she couldn't have that. So she put a stop to it. Thank goodness nothing ever came of it; she heard that he had dropped out of school early in the spring semester. She had been a new instructor and was very vulnerable, without tenure. Now she was an Assistant Professor on a tenure track. She felt a little safer in sampling the nubile flesh of the student body.

"You have to be very careful, Lily," Finch had said to her over drinks at Stache's one night. He had seen her admiring a couple of young students standing at the bar.

"Nice butts," she'd said.

"*Discreet,* Lily, you must be discreet. Listen to me. Your being on a tenure track is no protection at all. Shit, even when you get tenure, they can still can you for diddling a student."

"They have to have just cause," she said.

"That isn't just cause? Get serious. Administrators can get rid of you if they just don't like you, tenure or not. They'll find a way. They're experts at that."

"What are you telling me? Not to do it?"

"No, I wouldn't tell you that. You have your own mind. I'm just saying be exceedingly careful. You have to really *know* the student. I don't mean know in the ordinary sense; I mean be sure, as much as is possible, that they will not panic and make a to-do about it. There is a legal thing called "sexual harassment"; you don't hear very much about it, but believe me, administrators know about it, mainly because they have to protect themselves, predators that they are. Don't think that most of them don't sample the wares from time to time. I've heard that 'Big Hoss' can't keep his hands off them, both men and women. ("Big Hoss" Murphy was the Dean of Men, a crewcut ex-baseball player who went around punching everybody on the arm.) It goes on, Lily. All I'm saying is don't leave yourself vulnerable. I used to be quite active in that arena, but I was always acutely circumspect and vigilant with whom I chose. And another thing: I always let them seduce *me,* or think they were doing so. That levels the playing field. Makes them less likely to scream rape or something. Doesn't guarantee it, mind you, but it helps."

Lily took a sip of her gin and tonic. "That's great advice, Brass," she'd said.

Now she sat in her office, looking out the window at a mild, late September day, thinking of that conversation. The Florida heat of summer had tempered just a bit. There was a soft, balmy breeze coming through the window, smelling of the salty Gulf of Mexico forty miles away. She was thinking of another exchange she had had, this one with Owen Fielder, an instructor in the English department who had come to campus at the same time as Lily. He was in his second year, too, but he was still an instructor.

"I didn't even get a raise," he had told Lily.

"Well, that's tough shit, Owen," she'd said.

"You don't sound too unhappy about it," he'd said.

Lily did not care for Owen. He was skinny, with a flat top haircut that looked as though it had been trimmed with a razor so as to be as even as possible across the front. She had gone out with him once last year, and he had spent the evening in his apartment showing her pictures of girls he planned to date, coeds in the previous year's yearbook. He drove a little MG Midget that looked, in the front, exactly like him, with his wide, round eyes and evenly cut hair. His personality was grating to Lily. He had not been nice to her all last year, probably, she thought, because she was not impressed with his MG or her one date with him. She had refused a couple of half-hearted invitations after that, and he had stopped bothering her.

"I don't feel happy *or* unhappy about it, Owen," Lily said. "It's not my concern."

He was standing in her office door, looking down at her. She didn't bother to check out which parts of her anatomy he had been gaping at. He narrowed his eyes and smirked.

"Tell me, Lily," and he lowered his voice, "who do you have to fuck to get promoted to Assistant right off the bat, huh?"

"I don't know," she said. She shrugged.

"Finch?" he asked.

She didn't answer.

"Behn?" he asked.

Both, she thought.

"I bet both," he said. "And Doublet, too. And probably old fatso Dean Wallace. Uh-huh."

"Listen, Owen," she said, "who I fuck is my own business. Okay?"

"You didn't fuck *me,*" he said.

"No, and I can assure you, Mr. Fielder," she said, "that I never, under any circumstances, *will.*"

When the night in question arrived, there came a knock at Lily's door. When she opened it, there stood a nervous Sydney Polemus. His aftershave, or perhaps some cologne he was wearing, hit her in the face like a burst of wind.

"G…Good evening, Miss Putnam," he said, very formally. He stood in the doorway as if he were planted there.

She opened the door wider. "Why don't you come in," she said. He had a ring notebook under his arm and a ball point clipped in his shirt pocket. Maybe he thought she really *was* going to help him with his paper. Judging from his first paper of the semester, he needed little help. Should he want some, she would send him to the Writing Center. She had put on a pair of white short shorts that hugged her butt nicely, and she wore a Grateful Dead T shirt without a bra.

He came in and looked stiffly around. "Cool digs, Miss Putnam," he said. She could tell he could barely keep himself from gaping at her with his mouth hanging open, but he seemed to be struggling to keep his composure.

"Hardly," she said. "But thanks." It was an old apartment in an old, somewhat shabby building owned by Dr. Rock. (That's what everyone called him, because he was the lone professor of geology on the faculty. He was also the Grand Marshall, carrying the mace at all gowned convocations.) The apartment was partially furnished with furniture that reeked of the 1940s; she had bought a new couch and a comfortable king-sized bed from the same furniture store where Brasfield Finch had acquired his. She had admired it on her visits to his apartment; he lived in a much newer apartment building called The Florida Arms, with a balcony that looked out over the lush and verdant green of the Apalachicola River swamps. "Why don't we sit here?" she asked, indicating the couch.

"W...why not?" he said, sitting and opening the notebook on the spindly coffee table.

"Sydney..." she began.

"Syd," he said. "Call me Syd. That's what I go by."

"Okay," she said, "Syd. I've been thinking about it. I don't know if I should give you too much help on your paper. I mean, considering your aunt and that business and all."

"I'm sorry about all that, Miss Putnam," he said.

"Listen. When we're alone like this in my apartment, why don't you call me Lily?" she said.

"Really?" he asked.

"I'm not that much older then you, Syd. A year and a half ago I was still a student. (A *graduate* student, but she didn't make that distinction.) How old *are* you, by the way?"

"Nineteen," he said.

Ahhhhh, good, she thought. *That was one hurdle out of the way at least.*

"Let's just consider ourselves friends tonight, okay? Would you like a drink?"

"A what?"

"A drink. An adult beverage. Like liquor."

"I don't know if I should," he said.

"You do drink, don't you?"

"Yes mam. But mostly beer."

"I'm afraid I don't have any beer."

"A Tom Collins, then," he said.

"I'm sorry, Syd. I don't have any Tom Collins mix either. And, by the way, why don't we drop the 'mam' stuff, okay?"

"Okay, m… Okay."

"Have you ever had a martini?"

"No, I don't think I have. But I've heard of them. I seen them in a movie once."

"Saw," she said.

"*Saw*!" he said. "I wouldn't mind trying one."

"Give me a minute," she said. She went into her cramped kitchen, got out some ice that she had earlier busted out of the old metal, pull ice trays which she had had to struggle with. (Why didn't she just buy some new ones? She would have to put them on her list. Even into her second year of teaching she was still not used to having enough money to live on. Not much more than that, but she could still buy ice trays if she needed them.) She poured the gin and vermouth over the ice in a silver-plated shaker that had been a going away present from her good friend Sylvia Birch when she had left Atlanta. She made them five to one. She poured them into martini glasses that she had bought at a shop in Tallahassee and plopped an olive on a toothpick in each one. She still had plenty in the shaker, and she strained most of the ice out so as not to drown the remaining martinis.

She brought the drinks in on a plate. "Service fit for a king," she said, putting the plate on the coffee table.

"Wow," he said, "Why are you being so nice to me, Miss Putnam?"

"Syd!" she said sharply.

"I mean Lily," he said.

"I just like you, Syd," she said. "I mean, I enjoyed our talk in my office. It gets a little lonely for a single woman around here."

"I can't believe *that,* L…Lily. For a woman who looks like you do? Wow!" He picked up his martini and took a gulp and frowned. The toothpick had stuck him in the nose. Lily didn't know if he were frowning at the drink or about his nose.

"You're supposed to *sip* it, Syd. Like this." She sipped from her glass, showing him. She had made an excellent martini, worthy of Brasfield Finch himself. "Ahhhhh," she said.

He sipped. "Oh, that's good," he said. "I never tasted anything quite like it before." He sipped again.

"It's the drink of the gods, Syd," she said.

They sat for a while with their drinks. He finished his in record time. "Of the gods, huh?" he said.

"And there's plenty more where that one came from," she said. "Let me get the shaker."

He had another while she was finishing her first.

"Man, that's some good stuff," he said. After his second, his tongue was a little thick. She poured him another.

"Enjoy, Syd, but maybe you should slow down a little bit. I don't want you taking the lead out of your pencil." *Had she said that out loud?*

"Mam?" he asked.

"None of this 'mam' business, Syd. I meant," and she nodded toward his notebook on the coffee table "if you should decide to work on your paper."

"Miss Putnam…I mean Lily, I feel too good to work on any

paper. I mean, I feel *good*." He was savoring the martini now. He was a quick learner. She leaned back and put her arm across the back of the sofa. She folded her legs on the cushions. He was staring at them. He took another big swig of his drink.

"Don't *gulp*, Syd," she said.

He looked her in the eyes. He seemed so helpless at that point that she almost felt sorry for him. But she knew he would be amply rewarded. She would start off by giving him head, which he'd probably never experienced before.

"I brought a rubber," he blurted. As though he had known what she'd been thinking.

"Why, Mr. Polemus, whatever do you mean?" she said in her thickest Alabama accent, which she had almost, thank goodness, lost.

His eyes were swimmy. "It's Syd," he said.

"Of course. Syd."

"I'm sorry," he blundered, "I mean, I shouldn't have said…"

"No, that's all right. Do you mean you brought a condom?" He probably had one that was five years old in his wallet, with the foil all crushed, that he had bought from a machine in the men's room of a service station. But she had a good supply in her bedside table. She would substitute one of her new ones. In his shape he would never know the difference. She just hoped she hadn't given him too much liquor. But at his age, he would probably be randy as hell, even with three *more* martinis.

"Yeah," he said, "but I didn't mean…oh hell, I'm sorry. Shit. Shit. What a dunce I am."

"No, no, no, Syd, dear. It's just that a lady needs to be seduced, that's all." She gave him her most provocative smile. She patted the sofa cushion closer to her. "Come seduce me, darling, but be gentle," she said.

"You mean you're a v…v…virgin?!!" he said.

"Oh, no, no. Of course not. But I don't do this sort of thing very often." She could see his erection straining at his jeans. "Come. Seduce me," she said alluringly. She felt a bit silly saying those words, but she was trying to follow Brass's advice.

He moved over next to her. He put his arms around her and planted a kiss on her lips, his tongue probing her mouth. He had probably had plenty of experience in smooching. He caressed her breast. "Ohhh, you move fast," she said. He rubbed her crotch. His index finger slipped under her shorts and rubbed her clit through her panties. "Oh my god," she moaned, her breathing quickening. Maybe he *had* had more experience than she had thought. "Ohhhh," she sighed, "you know how to seduce a woman, Sydney. But I don't know...I don't know if I should go any further."

"Uh, Uh," he grunted. He was breathing fast, almost gasping. "We can't stop now," he squeezed out between pants.

"I don't want to stop," she wheezed. "But..." He continued to rub her clit. His finger slid under her bikini panties. "Oh my god," she said again. She could tell that she was already wet.

"Let's go into your bedroom," he puffed.

"Oh yes, Sydney, let's," she said. He heaved against her. *Don't let it go in your jeans*, she thought. *Please.*

He stood up, gripping her hand. He pulled her up. "You go ahead," she said, "I'll be right behind you."

"'Kay," he blubbered. He staggered some as he walked toward her bedroom door. He was already pulling his shirt off. Before she stood up she reached down and switched off the little mini tape recorder she had placed there. Just in case she had to convince him later that he had, indeed, been the seducer and she the seducee.

CHAPTER FOUR

Dean Wallace Jefferson left his office in Ferguson Hall and was strolling leisurely—or rather waddling slowly—across the quad toward the administration building and the office of John Stegall, the president. He wore a triple XL size blue pin stripe suit with a red striped tie. It was a pleasant, early October morning. There was not much seasonal change in that part of Florida, except for the summers, which were exceptionally hot and humid; fall, winter and spring were more temperate, with only a few quite cold days in January or February.

The administration building, Woodfin Hall, was the old music building, remodeled inside for offices. The president's suite consumed more than half the first floor, with the rest given over to a large board room with a round mahogany table, where the Board of Trust held their bi-annual meetings. Upstairs were the palatial offices of the deans of men and women, with smaller offices for the chair of the faculty senate, the business manager, and the director of buildings and grounds.

The student deans' offices in Woodfin were larger and more airy than Jefferson's office, which was off the lobby of Ferguson, which had once housed the entire administration on the first and second floors. Ferguson was also where the auditorium used for graduation and other large convocations was located. The lobby had had to be redone almost completely after the riot of high school and middle school students the previous spring, who had come to see the writer Lenora Hart, the speaker for the annual Senior Day Convocation, and for whom there was no room in the auditorium. It was just one more of President John Stegall's monumental snafus, and Dean Jefferson was now more convinced than ever that the old man had to go. During the previous academic year a disgruntled group of faculty had agitated for a vote of no confidence on Stegall, and Jefferson, in his role of chair of faculty meetings, had prevented it by declaring a somewhat chaotic meeting adjourned before the no confidence business could be completed. The dean had no doubt what the outcome would have been. He, himself, would have voted "no confidence." It was simply that he was not yet ready to make his own move for the office of president. He knew that some members of both the Board of Trust and the Faculty Senate would insist on a national search, and he would have to carefully cultivate local support as he put his name in with the various administrative personnel from around the country who would apply. He knew he already had the support of the "Harmon Mafia," a group of science and math professors who had been behind last year's effort at "no confidence," all of whom worked and taught in Harmon Hall.

Dean Jefferson breathed in the autumn air as he walked. He felt good; he had good prospects. When the time had come, he had refused to move to Woodfin, preferring instead to remain in the somewhat cramped quarters in Ferguson, with his corner office and a smaller office for his secretary. He liked the relative isolation of Ferguson; it was off the beaten path for most administrative doings on campus, and he could pick his own battles and campaigns. And he liked the relative privacy, which made it easy to carry on his affair with his secretary Alicia Martin, the wife of the manager of the local Walmart, on his office couch. Jefferson was a former professor of history, the department in which his wife Paulette taught and was now chair. The Dean felt that Lakewood was his; he had been there twenty years, and it was time he moved up another step. And then...who knew? Maybe the House of Representatives in Washington. Or governor. Or even senator. The possibilities were endless.

John W. Stegall sat in his enormous office behind his massive desk, doodling on a pad in front of him. He wore a blue pin stripe suit exactly like Jefferson's, except his looked as though it had been purchased in the junior department at J. C. Penney's, he was so small of stature. His imposing, heavy desk dwarfed him, and his secretary, Eloise Hoyle, was constantly reminding his to elevate his office chair whenever he had visitors.

He had little to do every day; he was grateful that things were calm on campus so far this semester. Last academic year had almost been the death of him. First there was the epidemic of streaking, students—both men and women—racing around the campus as naked as the day they were born, wearing only a ski mask. He had been appalled that such a thing could even happen in the world, much less on his own campus. A radio station in Tallahassee, on a show called "Morning Drive with Dick and Bubba," ran a daily tally on the number of streakings. It seemed that Lakewood and some college in the Northeast were neck and neck in the number of streaking events recorded. It was embarrassing and totally bad publicity for the college. Even the student newspaper, *The Floridian*, had run a two page center spread with un-retouched photos that had gone out to every high school in the state. Pubic hair everywhere. It was disgraceful. The governor, who was *ex officio* chairman of the Board of Trust, though he never attended meetings, had called Stegall up and reamed him out, as though it were all his fault.

Then there was a terrible gang rape on campus by a group of fraternity men, with attendant irate parents and threatened lawsuits. It had cost the college a pretty penny to settle with the girl's parents. Stegall and the college attorney had struggled mightily to keep the police out of it, for which they had been relatively successful—none of the men had had to stand trial and go to jail. But they had not succeeded in blocking the publicity; TV stations from all over the state showed up to do stories on the rape. There was another round of bad publicity, for which Stegall was blamed, because he had been powerless to stop the streaking—the girl who was raped was indeed streaking herself. It was a nightmare.

Then there had been the fiasco with Lenora Hart, not to mention the dreadful attempt to get the faculty to vote "no confidence" in him, which was ridiculous, since he, himself, was fully confident that he was the best president the college had ever had. Thank goodness that came to nothing, as it should have. But the Lenora Hart business! He had wound up in the hospital with a heart attack, though his ignorant doctors had refused to acknowledge that, claiming instead that he had suffered extreme tension and anxiety, which had resulted in exceptional exhaustion.

He had been agitating for years to have Lenora Hart come to the campus. She was one of America's most endeared writers, who, years ago, had written a young adult's novel called *To Lynch a Wild Duck*, which had crossed over and become a national best seller and had earned Hart the Pulitzer Prize. She was Florida's own, making her home in Siesta Key, in the Gulf off Sarasota. Her novel was one of the most popular books ever published, each year selling millions of copies worldwide (more, even—by some estimations—than *The Holy Bible*). It was taught in middle schools, high schools and colleges all over the United States. Stegall had even, against his better judgment, enlisted the aid of his drunken writer-in-residence, Brasfield Finch, to lure the woman to Lakewood, since she was loath to make public appearances and was notoriously reclusive and would never sign copies of her famous and beloved book. Finch was a friend of hers, so he said, and, indeed, a letter from him had proven to be—much to Stegall's later regret—the thing that had finally gotten her to accept.

She had been rude, crude and altogether unpleasant, performing a drunken, vulgar and profane spectacle of herself at the annual Senior Day Convocation last spring. The event always drew hundreds of parents. And Stegall had made the mistake (and he readily admitted this, though he had done it with the very best of intentions) of sending out a blanket invitation to every middle and high school in the Florida Panhandle, and students and teachers had shown up in droves to meet the famous writer and get their copies of *To Lynch a Wild Duck* autographed. Of course there had not been enough room in Ferguson Auditorium for them all, and the students had rioted like hoodlums, egged on by Miss Hart's inebriated behavior.

When Dean Jefferson had settled his aggregate largeness into a visitor's chair and had exchanged pleasantries with the president, he got right to the point.

"Have you given any more thought to retirement, John?" he asked.

"I beg your pardon?" Stegall said, frowning.

"Retirement. After all, you *are* getting a little long in the tooth."

"I don't know what you mean, Wallace. I'm only seventy years old. Seventy is the new forty, I read somewhere."

The dean chuckled. "I agree, John," he said, "but the state encourages retirement at sixty five."

"I know," Stegall said, "but it is not required. I have forty one years in the system, and a couple more would be nice. I have the assurance of the board of trust that they will elevate my salary nicely, to give me a good retirement pension. I have my eye on a new sailboat over in Pensacola." He smiled.

The dean smiled back. "That's very good, John," he said.

"I have absolutely *no* intention of retiring before then," Stegall said firmly.

This may be more difficult that I had imagined, Jefferson thought. He paused for a long moment. "John," he said, "remember the no confidence vote that I saved you from last year."

Stegall snorted. "*You* saved me? Get serious, Wallace. This faculty would *never* have voted no confidence in me, and you know it."

"Well, there *is* talk," the dean said.

"Talk? Talk is cheap."

"I mean, the Hart business last year, the rape and the streaking, all that," Jefferson said. He leaned over and tapped the president's mammoth desk. "The buck stops here, John."

Stegall snorted again. "I have *utter* confidence in my confidence!" he said.

"Still, we wouldn't want it to come to that. A vote, I mean."

"Bring it on! If that's what they want! This bunch of pinheads doesn't have the balls to do it!" Stegall looked startled at what he had said. "Excuse my French," he added.

"I wouldn't be too sure of that, John. From my vantage point, there is much unrest among the faculty."

"That bunch in Harmon Hall," Stegall said.

"No, it's more wide-spread than that. I'm just warning you, my friend. Perhaps a retirement would be more pleasant than a repeat of what happened last spring."

"We won't be inviting Lenora Hart again, I can assure you of that."

"No, I mean the no confidence vote. That I successfully aborted...even if you don't remember it that way. I can't guarantee you it would work out the same way if it happened again. It could get ugly. Think of your reputation, John. Your legacy here."

"My reputation is *sterling*," the president said haughtily. "What are you getting at, Wallace? I don't like the sound of this."

"I only have your welfare at heart, John," the dean said, "nothing else."

"Well, I thank you for your concern. But I am quite capable of taking care of myself."

"I know you are, John. Still..."

"What are you implying, Wallace?"

"I'm not *implying* anything. You are my president, and my friend. I am just alerting you to the danger in the swamp, because I am your dean. I see that as part of my job description. That's all."

"Well, all right," Stegall said. He crossed his arms across his narrow chest. Jefferson could tell he had pumped up his desk chair so that he sat taller than his visitor.

"That's all," Dean Jefferson said again.

Walking back across the quad to his office, the dean was thinking and ruminating. Stegall would be hard to convince to retire gracefully. He was weak, and silly, but he was a very stubborn man. *I guess this is going to have to be a bloodless coup,* the dean thought, as he waddled across the sidewalk. He smiled to himself. *Or maybe a* bloody *one. Come hell or high water, and if the Creek don't rise*—as a professor of American history, Jefferson knew that the saying referred to the Creek Indian Nation, a warlike tribe that had been defeated by General Andrew Jackson at the Battle of Horseshoe Bend, and not creeks, as most people thought—*he would be in the president's office by spring!*

President Stegall sat doodling on his pad. He had lowered his chair so he would be more comfortable at his desk. He, as well, was thinking hard. Not for the first time, he thought: *that son of a bitch wants my job!*

CHAPTER FIVE

Lily heard a soft, polite tapping at her open office door, and when she looked up from the paper she was grading with her trusty red ballpoint, there stood J. J. Underwood (or J. J. Underwear, as the students called him), the director of the college theater. He was a tall, thin man with an unruly shock of blonde hair who spoke in an extremely affected manner.

"Miss Putnam?" he said, with a slightly British lilt.

"Yes?" she said, not too pleasantly. It was the first time she had seen him since a very icky and distasteful scene with him and his wife Tulah, when they had invited her to their apartment to read privately for the part of Maggie in *Cat on a Hot Tin Roof,* and the evening, fueled by too much alcohol, had culminated with Tulah—who had been reading the part of Brick—kissing Lily full on the lips with probing tongue, while both of them caressed her bottom in a three way embrace. Lily had indignantly left, and had not spoken with the man since. It was not that she was opposed to three ways; she was just particular about with whom she engaged in them.

"Now Lily, I want to profusely apologize again for what happened last year when you read for Maggie," he said. "Tulah just got carried away reading Brick, and, well, you were such a perfect Maggie, and all that. It's a shame it didn't work out. Lindsey Pruett was a pretty good Maggie, but she could not possibly be as good as you would have been."

"Lindsey Pruett? Freddy the Falcon?" Lily asked.

"Why yes," he said. "I think she was supposed to be anonymous in that role. She couldn't speak while in costume. But she was good. She is a good little actress."

"Yes, well, what can I do for you this morning, J. J.?"

"May I come in?" he said, entering without invitation. He moved like a giant praying mantis. He settled himself in her visitor's chair and smiled at her. He wore a loose white cotton shirt that tied at the neckline with a string.

"Lily," he said, and paused, "I hope you don't mind if I call you Lily."

"Of course not," Lily said.

"I hope you will listen to me before you say no," he said. "I know we got off on the wrong foot with the Maggie audition, but I want you to know that our big fall production, to be done the week before Christmas holidays, is *A Doll's House*." She did not respond, and he held his hand palm out toward her. "Don't say anything until I'm finished, okay?"

"I wasn't going to say anything," she said.

"In any case, Nancy Magill, who teaches voice in the music department, has agreed to play Mrs. Linde. Our new assistant professor in theater—I don't know if you've met him—Maxfield Tingle is his name, will play Torvald. He is a fine, mature actor for a young man."

"Yes, I remember him from the new faculty reception at Flower Hill," she said. He was nice looking, but she had thought him a little too delicate and subdued for her taste. Maybe she had been wrong. It would not be the first time she had misjudged a man.

"And Norman Lawrence, our former director of theater at Lakewood, has agreed to come out of retirement to play Dr. Rank. We will fill the minor roles with students. That, of course, leaves only Nora." He peered curiously at her. "Lily, dear," he said, "you would be the absolute perfect Nora!"

"I thought I would have been the absolute perfect Maggie," she said.

"When you think about it, Lily, they are very similar women, very strong women. It has been observed many times that the liberation of women began in 1879, with the slamming of that door when Nora leaves Torvald, in the premier of *A Doll's House* at the Royal Theater in Copenhagen, Denmark on December 21st of that year.

That was the beginning. Modern women owe so much to Ibsen, and *A Doll's House* is still a dramatic mantra for modern women. And Nora is the ultimate heroine of feminism. Actresses are honored to play her, and many of the finest actresses in the world have done so over the years. You could take your own place in that long line of performers, Lily, dear."

"But I'm not an actress," Lily said.

"Oh, but you are. You were so convincing just *reading* for Maggie that Tulah and I...well..."

"Let's just don't go there, okay?" Lily said.

"Fine," he said. He was looking pleadingly at her. It was hard to tell when he was sincere and when he was acting. Maybe they had merged over his years to become the same thing. "Will you at least consider it?" he asked, "please?"

She thought a moment. She made a snap decision. "Yes, I'll consider it," she said.

His face lit up like a Christmas tree. "Oh, Lily, you don't know how happy you have made this old director this morning."

"I said I'd consider it, not that I'd do it. I'll have to think about it."

"Of course. Take all the time you want. But you are my Nora, Lily, I know you are," he said.

"Well, we'll see," said Lily.

Lily was very tempted to take the part. Her only real hesitation was working with J. J. She had long harbored a secret desire to act. When she had been a senior at Birmingham-Southern, she had tried out for *The Fantasticks* and had won the part of Henry, the old actor. Her boyfriend at the time had tried out for Mortimer, the old actor's Indian side-kick, and had also won the part. They had had a wonderful time with their English accents and Mortimer's dramatic, repeated dying on stage. They had had to disguise Lily's figure under her Elizabethan costume, and that had been difficult, but they had managed. As Henry, Lily had "brought down the house." She was that funny. (Only later did she realize that the old actor *always* "brought down the house.) The other players and the crew were warm and welcoming to her, though she was an English major and had had zero experience on the stage. It had been an experience that Lily had immensely enjoyed.

Also, during her Birmingham-Southern years, she had worked part time in the box office at the *Ritz Movie Palace* downtown. (She had to work to help her parents supplement their expenses, since Southern was an expensive private college, but the best in the state, and that's what Lily wanted.) She had always liked the movies, and the company that owned the *Ritz* also owned *The Alabama*, a much larger theater on Third Avenue, and *The Empire*, also in downtown Birmingham. Lily had a pass, so she could see every first run movie that came to town. And that, too, had whetted her appetite for acting.

She had briefly toyed with the idea of changing her major; but she was nearing graduation and quite busy. She had already applied to graduate schools and had been accepted at Emory. And in graduate school, she was too busy studying to entertain any ambition for the stage. She had not given it much thought since her undergraduate days. She had been sorely tempted by the role of Maggie in last year's production of the Tennessee Williams play, but her experience with J. J. and Tulah had severely soured that idea. Now she felt she was better prepared to deal with the Underwoods. (Tulah was the costumer for the college theater.) She had checked out a collection of Ibsen's plays from the library and had re-read *A Doll's House*. She *loved* the play, and she agreed with J. J. Underwood about one thing: she was perfect for the role of Nora. And she felt that she could do the part justice. So this was a chance to get back on the stage and re-experience the thrill of performing before a live audience. She just hoped she was not making a terrible mistake. But she bit the bullet and called J. J. and told him she would take the part.

"Oh, Lily, dear, you make me very happy. You make the *theatrical world* very happy!"

"I wouldn't go quite that far, J. J.," she said.

Underwood called a cast meeting and a read-through; they all met in the college theater, a 400 seat state of the art playhouse upstairs in Palmer Hall, which housed the drama department. J. J. sat on the edge of the stage, the cast and crew facing him from the center of the first two rows. He wore what looked to Lily like women's black tights under one of his loose-fitting white cotton blouses that tied at the neck. He looked every bit "the director," which amused the hell out of Lily, but she kept a straight face. Underwood distributed playing scripts and number 2 yellow pencils. "Make any notes on your speeches in pencil, and later on your blocking notes the same, so they can easily be changed. See this?" he said, pointing dramatically to an eraser on a pencil. "Do you know what this is for?"

"Shit, yeah," came a voice from among the crew on the second row.

"Just what I'd expect," said J. J. He pointed to one of the boys. "This, people, in case any of you don't know him, is Leon Miata, our lighting director. Miata, like the car. I don't know if that's his real name or not; perhaps Mr. Miata has already chosen his stage name for his theatrical career." There were titters and giggles. Lily thought she remembered teaching him in a trailer section of English 102, way last fall. The section was for repeaters of the second half of freshman English. But she had had so many students she couldn't be sure. The name was familiar, but she didn't think she'd ever seen the boy before in her life. Maybe he hadn't attended class and had dropped the course. Drama majors, while lively—even flamboyant—were notoriously terrible students.

"Let me first introduce our faculty members, our major players. I have heard your grumbling, and I know some of you are not happy about my decision to cast the parts closer to age, with more experienced actors. But students have all the other parts. And we must all learn all we can from every production we're in. Remember, 'there are no small parts…'" He paused.

"'…only small actors,'" the students said in unison, with many groans and snorts at the cliché.

"The reason it is a cliché, my dear young friends, is that it is *true,*" Underwood continued. "The success of a play is only as strong as its weakest performer. Remember that. Even if you are cast as only a walk-on, you must play it with the utmost seriousness, bringing to bear on it all your talents as an actor. If you cannot do that, you let the rest of the cast and crew down. You let the *play* down. You let *me* down. And you let *Mr. Ibsen,* God rest his soul, down."

There were murmurs of assent. Lily could barely contain herself. She would have to work very hard not to laugh out loud.

"First, our Nora," he said. "Most of you know Miss Putnam. Miss Putnam had great success playing the old Shakespearean actor in a production of *The Fantasticks* when she was an undergraduate. (He had asked them all to fill out a sheet with their vital statistics, sizes, and acting experience; Lily had said nothing about her "success" as Henry.) She is our perfect Nora, and I know we will all enjoy working with her. Next, on the end of the row, is Nancy Magill, from the music department, who will play Mrs. Linde. Nancy has extensive experience in opera, so she is no stranger to the stage."

"Call me Lil," Nancy said.

"Pardon?" Underwood said.

"I said call me Lil. That's what I call myself."

"But ever since you've been at Lakewood, Miss Magill, everyone has known you as Nancy."

"I know," she said, "but call me Lil."

Over the years some people had called Lily "Lil"; even a few members of the faculty had called her that. She wondered if the exchange were some kind of slap to her. *I'm being paranoid*, she thought.

"Lil Magill it is, then," Underwood said. "Sitting next to Lil is Max Tingle, whom you all know—some of you are in his acting class, and two of you are in his sophomore speech course, but more about you later—one of our newest faculty members in the theater department, who will play Torvald. Max has extensive experience on the stage, most recently as Nick in a dinner theater production of *Who's Afraid of Virginia Woolf* at the Waves Playhouse in Grayton Beach, Florida. And our own esteemed director-emeritus, a legend here at Lakewood, Norman Lawrence, has agreed to come out of retirement to play Dr. Rank." The man stood up and waved theatrically with one hand, as if he were taking a bow. Lily thought he was about seventy; he had a protruding belly and his jowls and under-eye bags—in fact, his entire face—sagged loosely. He resembled The Cowardly Lion in *The Wizard of Oz*. Then he growled, "I've got my eyes on you, Underwood."

"Good one, Norm," J. J. said, and grinned a stiff, constricted smile.

This should be good, thought Lily.

J. J. coughed discreetly into his elbow. He looked around as though he had forgotten what he was going to say next. "And, of course," he said, after a minute, "our student players. Jim Krim will play Krogstad. Jim is a senior theater major. He is a veteran, a returning student who played Big Daddy in last year's production of *Cat on a Hot Tin Roof*. Sitting next to him is Dorothy Fields, who will play Anne-Marie, the nanny. This is her first time onstage with us, though she has worked very hard on crew in the past. And playing the Helmer children, Bob, Emmy and Ivar, three of our freshman majors who, though small in stature, are large in talent. Heh, heh." He pointed to the three, sitting together on the front row at the end. The two boys who were playing Bob and Ivar looked much younger than the average freshman. The girl was diminutive; she sat upright in the seat in a little pink dress. She wore white socks with tiny black Mary Jane shoes; her feet did not touch the floor. Lily looked at her face; her features were all scrooched up. *My God*, thought Lily, *the girl is a midget!* "Lucille McCulley will play Helen, the maid, and Jim Vickery will play the porter," Underwood went on. "That's our cast, my dear young friends. Our stage manager will be Lucas Haas, Lucas, stand up. Most of you know him. He will be second in command to me…he will be your boss when you're onstage. He will be the one wearing the headset during rehearsals and performances. Be friendly to him, you will need him." Most of the students laughed knowingly. "Back to our two sophomore non-majors from Mr. Tingle's speech class. They, Liz and Marie, will be your prop mistresses. We will recruit prompters from among our majors on a rotating basis. Ditto with the house. As most of you know, Anne Kemp, our debate coach, volunteers as house manager for our productions, and she will assemble her own crew for programs, advanced ticket sales and reservations, publicity, and the box office. Have I covered everything? No, of course not. Heh, heh. Our set crew. Once again it will be headed by Wayne Beatty, and he, too, will recruit volunteers. *A Doll's House* is a simple one set piece. The set will not be overly demanding. Wayne has already contacted West Side Antiques for the loan of furniture. Once we get that all in place, and you have memorized your lines, we will do the final blocking. I will post a rehearsal schedule. Friends, I warn you. We will be off-book in two weeks. So get busy committing those lines to memory. Then we can get down to the serious business of acting the play. It's going to be a great production. Are there any questions?"

"Yes," Jim Krim said. "Who's hosting the cast party?" There was much jovial laughter.

"I suppose Tulah and I will once again do the honors," Underwood said, "unless…" And he glanced at the adult cast members. "…unless we have another volunteer."

"I'll speak to Annette about it," Norman Lawrence said. "We used to have some wing-dingers back in the olden days. Back during the Punic Wars."

"Hey, that's a quote from *Virginia Woolf*," Maxfield Tingle said.

"That it is, young man," Lawrence said.

"I must have heard it ten thousand times. The guy who played George…"

"…Yes, well," J. J. said, interrupting, "thanks, Norman. And give my best to your lovely Annette. Are there any other questions?" No one asked another one. Tingle looked miffed at being shut off in mid-story. "Then get out your playing scripts and let's have a read-through. Don't bother with acting overmuch, we'll just read. We'll have a couple more of these, one in which we'll read the lines as fast as we possibly can. We'll *race* through it. You'll be surprised at how much of a grasp you can get of the rhythm of the play that way." Some of the assembly nodded purposely.

Two weeks? Lily would have to enlist Brass or Willow to help her with her lines. She didn't remember any problems at all in learning the old actor's lines, but that had been a much smaller part. Now she was the *lead!*

"All right," Underwood said. He began reading the stage directions at the beginning of act one. "A room, tastefully furnished etc. etc. There is a bell offstage in the hall, and after a second the door— THAT DOOR—is opened. Nora enters, in outdoor dress, followed by a porter with a Christmas tree." He paused. "All right. They are met by the maid Helen. Nora?"

Lily read: "Hide the Christmas tree carefully, Helen. Be sure the children do not see it until this evening, when it is dressed. (To the porter.) How much?"

Jim Vickery read: "Sixpence."

Lily read: "There is a shilling. No. Keep the change."

"Very good," Underwood said. "You see, right at the beginning of the play, Ibsen establishes that Nora is something of a spendthrift, rather loose with money. This will become a central conflict with Torvald as the drama progresses. All right, read on," he said.

Brass Finch readily agreed to help Lily with her lines. They met at his apartment, fixed themselves drinks (he Scotch on the rocks, her gin and tonic) and sat on his sofa with the playing script in front of them. Brass read Torvald's lines.

"I guess that Tingle fellow is perfect for this part," Brass said. "When I met him I thought he was a little wimpy. I couldn't believe that young a man could be that stooped."

"Stooped?" Lily said. "Is that what's wrong with him?"

"Haven't you noticed? I thought there might be an issue with his neck or something."

"*That's* what it is," Lily said. "Yep, he'll do Torvald justice."

"As you will Nora, Lily dear, I have no doubt. I'm really looking forward to seeing this play. I long ago gave up on college theatricals. I said to myself, 'Lord, deliver me from anything *amateur*!,' excluding of course certain sporting events such as Little League baseball, of which I am quite fond, though I never had a son myself. Pity."

"Brass, you are too much," Lily said. "I learn something new about you every day!"

Lily worked on learning her lines by herself in her apartment. She found herself running them in her mind while she was at work. She would have to try hard not to have the play be too much of a distraction. Of course, doing the show would eliminate any time she might have spent on her dissertation, but she didn't care. She was going to have fun.

"I can't believe you let yourself get hooked up with those dreadful Underwoods," Willow said when she came over to Lily's apartment to read Mrs. Linde.

"Well, I had my real doubts," Lily said. "Still do, as a matter of fact. But I want to play Nora, Willow. As a feminist, I think the role is important."

"So do I," Willow said. "I just hope that J. J. Underwood has the sense to understand that."

"I think he does, Willow. I think you'll be proud of the play."

"I'll certainly come to see it. I don't care much for college plays, quit going years ago. But I'll certainly come to see *you*."

"That's almost exactly what Brass said," Lily said.

"He did? I would think Mr. Finch would be too much in his cups by curtain time to watch *any* play."

"He doesn't drink as much as people think," Lily said.

"Come now, Lily my dear, come now," Willow said.

CHAPTER SIX

Dean Wallace Jefferson had his secretary get Dr. Garcia Russo on the telephone. Russo had been the ring leader in last year's attempt to get a vote of no confidence on John Stegall. He had sent out a series of inflammatory broadsides that were quite insulting to Stegall. Russo was an associate professor in the math department who had tried repeatedly in recent years to get promoted to full professor. He had once angrily accused Dean Jefferson of racial and ethnic discrimination, claiming that his grandparents had emigrated from Cuba.

"So sue me," Jefferson had said; he had wanted to tell Russo that the reason he wasn't promoted was because he was an all-around unpleasant person, a pluperfect asshole, one of the most obnoxious and disagreeable members of the faculty. "I have utterly no idea of the ethnic origins of your family, Dr. Russo," Jefferson had said, "and it wouldn't matter to me if I did."

"H…hello," Russo said, answering the phone call suspiciously.

The dean knew that Alicia Martin had said to him, "I have a call for you from Dean Jefferson."

"This is Wallace Jefferson," the dean said jovially.

"I know who it is," Russo said. He sounded disgusted. Jefferson chewed on his lower lip. Russo had once, during a faculty meeting, when Jefferson was assuring the faculty that the administration was doing everything in its power to get them all a raise for the next year, shouted, interrupting him, "You're a *liar,* Wallace!"

"I was wondering, Garcia," Jefferson said, "if you still had your group going. You know the bunch you called 'The Harmon Mafia.' Ha, ha."

"Why do you ask?" Again, with much suspicion.

"I was wondering if I might meet with you all next time you get together."

"*You*? Meet with *us*?"

"Yes."

"You're the enemy, Wallace. Why should we meet with you?"

"Oh, but Garcia, I'm *not* your enemy. I'm on your side."

"*Our* side? You sure had a funny way of showing it last year!"

"Frankly, I think you misread the situation," the dean said.

"How so?"

"I just didn't think the time was ripe."

There was a long pause. "But you do now, huh? Listen, Wallace, why should I believe you? This is some kind of trick, isn't it? I get it, infiltrate the enemy camp and get the dope, right?"

"You're not my enemy, Garcia. We are allies. Let me meet with your people and explain myself."

"My people, huh? You make it sound like we're some kind of undesirable minority."

"Oh, no, not at all. I just mean your group."

"What do you know about my '*group*?'"

"Not much, really. I just know that some of you people over in Harmon tried to do something decent for the school last spring, and it didn't work out."

"Something decent?"

"Yes. To get rid of Stegall."

There was another long pause. "I don't get it," Russo said, "you mean you want another no confidence vote?"

"Better than that." Jefferson leaned back, patting his belly. He set the hook. "A coup."

"A coup? What the hell are you talking about?"

"Run the son-of-a-bitch out. Take over his office. Get rid of him for good."

"And you...you? Shit, Wallace, you want to replace him." He laughed. "I get it now."

"Well, what do you think? Let me meet with the mafia. We can all do it together."

"I don't know. I don't know if they would go for it."

"At least invite me to talk to them."

Another pause. After a minute, "Okay. I'll get them together."

"Good. Just let me know when. Where does your group...uh, meet?"

"We usually get together at R. D. Wettermark's house. Have a few drinks. But, hell, R. D. said he wasn't going to supply the booze any longer. Tight bastard. He poured little lady-like drinks, anyhow."

"Tell you what. I'll bring the bottle. Hell, I'll bring *two*. What do you fellows drink?"

"Bourbon. That's the drink of southern men, ain't it?"

"I suppose so," Jefferson said, smiling to himself. "And, Garcia, I pour liberally. That's about the only thing I do that could be labeled with that word."

"Good. Okay then. I'll call you?"

"Just call Alicia," Jefferson said, "she'll put it on my calendar."

"All right," Garcia said. He put the phone back on its cradle. *Call his secretary*, Garcia thought. *Shit, the son-of-a-bitch was still every inch an administrator. The Harmon Mafia would all have to have each other's backs.*

Wallace Jefferson had already enlisted the support of Brandon Briggs, the college attorney and member of the board of trust, along with two other members, Susan Cranston Bart, an alumna from Fort Myers, and Willie Long, an attorney in Jupiter, to have himself appointed interim president should John Stegall become incapacitated in any way. (Of course, this was still a minority of the board; but Wallace felt sure that their influence would convince the other members, most of whom were senile or completely clueless as to how a university should be run.) As interim, he would have something of an inside track when the time came for the national search, for which Jefferson thought himself fully qualified: his PhD was from the University of Georgia, and he had taught there for two years before accepting a position as Assistant Professor of History at Lakewood College, where he had risen through the ranks to become first department chairman (a position which his wife Paulette, also a Georgia PhD, now held) and then Dean of the College. He had published one book entitled *Sherman: Merchant of Terror* (University of South Carolina Press, 1967) and, during the sixties, had served as president of the Barber County White Citizens' Council. He was a scholar of The Civil War, his hero being Thomas Jonathan "Stonewall" Jackson. He had given several papers at the Southern Historical Association and had published essays on Jackson, The Battle of Atlanta, and the Siege of Vicksburg. His scholarly credentials were impeccable, and he had been—in his own humble estimation—the best dean Lakewood had ever had.

And if his scheme worked, Stegall would become—sooner rather than later—incapacitated. The man had been on the verge of a breakdown since the past fall, when the epidemic of streaking had swept through the student body. Subsequent events—a rape, a disastrous visit to the campus by the appallingly abominable woman Lenora Hart, for both of which Stegall bore full responsibility, and an attempt by a faction of the faculty to force a vote of no confidence in him—had driven him further toward the brink. Jefferson felt that it would take very little to tip the scales. Stegall was an unstable man, and the dean planned to take full advantage of it.

The dean relaxed with his drink in the den of R. D. Wettermark, a professor of biology. R. D.'s den, or his "man cave" as he called it, was in the back of his house and was decorated with an Auburn motif, with action photos of Auburn football games on the walls. Auburn was where Wettermark had earned his PhD. There was a large television set. Over the bar hung a huge blue and orange "War

Eagle" banner. Jefferson had brought two quarts of Maker's Mark, and the other men were impressed.

"That's a step up from Early Times," Donald Katz, another biology teacher, said.

"What the hell's wrong with Early Times?" Wettermark asked harshly.

"Nothing. I just meant…"

"It was *free*, Don. I don't remember you…"

"Get over it, R. D.," Katz said. "I just meant that Maker's Mark is really good stuff."

"So is Early Times," Wettermark said, pouting.

"Gentlemen, gentlemen," said Russo, "behave yourselves. We have a guest."

Jefferson nodded as the other men turned their full attention to him. They were Russo and Alexander Daniels, from math, and Wettermark, Katz, and Fred C. Dobbs, from biology. Lyman Pershing, from physics, had joined them for the first time.

"This is it?" Jefferson asked.

"Well, we sometimes have more from time to time," Russo said. "Lyman, for example, was recruited by Dobbs. We have plenty of support."

"That's what I'm counting on," Jefferson said.

"Well…?" Katz said.

Jefferson outlined his course of action to them. He told them about Briggs, Bart, and Long. He tried to explain his thinking.

"What I want to know is," Russo interrupted him, "is what's in this for us?"

"Of course, of course," the dean said. "First, you will get rid of Stegall, something you all want, right? And second, when I am president, all my loyal supporters will be well taken care of."

"You mean promotions, salary?" Wettermark asked.

"Yes."

"What about tenure?" Lyman Pershing asked. His tongue was already thick, though Jefferson surmised he'd had only one drink, two at the most.

"Certainly. All that. My allies and I will run the institution," Jefferson said.

"What about the black helicopters?"

"Dr. Pershing…" the dean began.

"Yeah, what about *them*?" Wettermark said.

"The Pentagon…" Jefferson began again.

"You believe the goddamn Pentagon?!" Russo exclaimed.

"Gentlemen, gentlemen, if I could do something about the black helicopters I would. In the meantime…"

"Let the son-of-a-bitch speak!" Katz interjected.

Pershing stood up, grasping his throat. "I feel drunk," he said, "the son-of-a-bitch put something in that fancy whiskey of his."

"You feel drunk because you gulped two glasses of my 'fancy whiskey,'" Jefferson said. He was becoming more and more irritated with their behavior. *My God,* he thought, *these people are crazy. But then,* he supposed, *all radical revolutionaries were crazy.*

Just then, Pershing, still grasping his throat, fell to the floor in a heap.

"This is taking it too far, Dr. Pershing," Jefferson said. "Get up from there. You're drunk!"

"Hell, the bastard's been drinking all day," Katz said.

"Yeah. He's an alcoholic," Dobbs said.

"Why, then, did you invite him?" the dean asked.

"Because there," Dobbs said, pointing to the man passed out on the floor, "but by the grace of God, go I."

"I'd leave God out of it, if I were you," Jefferson said.

"It is well known, Dean Jefferson, that the Russians are massing an entire army, with tanks and artillery, along the Mexican border," said R. D. Wettermark. "The helicopters are their spy planes. Thousands of people have seen them."

"And what do you expect me to do about that?" the dean asked.

"Nothing," Katz said.

"Then why bring it up?"

"He's right," Katz said, "let's get back on task. What makes you think you'll get the permanent appointment? Even with those board of trust bozos in your corner."

"I will, Donald. Don't you worry," said Jefferson.

Willow Behn sometimes ate lunch in the student cafeteria—known affectionately by all on campus as The Caf—especially on Thursdays, when they served some of the best baked chicken breasts that she'd ever tasted. The portions were large (she usually got, along with the chicken, creamed spinach and field peas, with a big chunk of cornbread) and she could carry half of it home with her for her evening meal. Willow lived alone in an old house at the edge of campus that had been converted into three apartments. She shared the house with Joan Hudson, art, and Lucille Willard, history, two slightly older single women.

As Willow put her tray down on a mercifully empty faculty table and sat, spreading her paper napkin on her lap, she was recalling an incident from the past year when she had been startled by a naked coed who came streaking through the Caf at lunchtime wearing nothing but sneakers and a ski mask. She had seen several more streakers during that period of time when the practice became rampant on campus: out the window of her classroom, on the sidewalk in front of her apartment house where she had been sitting on the porch one evening having a glass of wine with Miss Hudson and Dr. Willard—that one a male—and once during a performance in the concert hall of the new music building, at an annual recital that was performed by Marilyn Street and Calvin Meyer, married duo pianists who were Lakewood's artists in residence and who toured the Southeast in their long black Cadillac pulling a trailer with their two matching grand pianos inside. The girl who had streaked their concert—entering stage left and circling in front of the duo, shimmying for a few seconds and then exiting stage right—was a tall blonde, judging from the tint of her pubic hair; she, too, wore a ski mask. Willow was almost certain, from her demeanor, height, and bearing, that she was a girl in Willow's Victorian Novels class. The girl had written her paper on Hardy's *Tess of the d'Urbervilles.*

Before she had taken two bites, Fred C. Dobbs sat down across from her. Dobbs taught biology and had a huge belly that strained against his belt line; he wore wide, red suspenders with brass clips. His cheeks were chubby and his dark eyes were beady.

"Morning, Willow," he said, "or is it afternoon?"

"Take your pick," Willow said shortly. She did not care overmuch for Dobbs, and she was disappointed to have her solitary lunch so quickly disrupted.

Dobbs held out his plate with two plump chicken breasts. "Look, Ja…"

"Jayne Mansfield," she interrupted. "How many more times are you going to make that joke, Dr. Dobbs? By my count, that's three hundred and twelve."

"Aw, Willow, now don't tell me you don't like titties," he said, smirking. Her eyes narrowed and she put down her fork, glaring at him. He held out his palm toward her. Remembering the time last year when he had said something similar to her and she had hurled a half-eaten, creamed-spinach-soaked chicken breast and hit him square in the face, he said quickly, "All right, all right. Sorry. I was out of line."

"When, Dr. Dobbs," she asked dryly, "have you ever been *in* line?"

Dobbs chuckled. "You're too much, Willow," he said, smiling good naturedly.

Willow sliced and ate her chicken breast without replying. They ate in silence for a few moments. The Caf was getting more and more crowded with noisy students. Willow didn't mind the noise. The fact was that she liked to walk into her classroom to boisterous chattering rather than to dead, sulky silence, the latter state of affairs being a sure sign of a drear and apathetic group that would be boring to teach.

"Well," Dobbs said, after a few minutes of chewing and swallowing, "I heard some scuttlebutt on campus." He wiped his mouth with his wrinkled napkin and took a sip of his iced tea.

"I'm sure you did," Willow said shortly, not wanting to hear the latest faculty gossip. That bored her, too; she much preferred spending her time with her books or with her friend and sometimes lover Lily Putnam. She even had to admit to herself that she rather, at times, enjoyed the liveliness that the appallingly beastly and drunken Brasfield Finch brought to the English department.

"I heard," Dobbs said, smacking his thick lips (Willow had once heard a student refer to him as "old Liver Lips.") and leaning toward her so as to lower his voice, "that our esteemed president, *the dwarf,* is on his way out."

"Says who?" Willow asked.

"Oh, I heard it around," he said smugly.

Willow peered at him across the table. After a pause, she said, "Is that dreadful Russo getting up to his old tricks again?"

"No, I heard it from higher up than that."

"Spare me," Willow said.

"Okay. I'm really not at liberty to tell you who, anyway."

"Good," she said. She concentrated on her chicken and her creamed spinach. Willow absolutely *loved* the Caf's creamed spinach.

"Anyhoo, that's what I heard," Dobbs said.

"You said that, Dr. Dobbs," Willow said.

Lily and Finch, after work one late afternoon, walked downtown to Stache's to have a couple of drinks. Stache's was a funky bar that catered to young faculty and students. Finch liked it because they made a more than adequate martini and poured a hefty Scotch on the rocks. It was in an old house with a porch around three sides for outdoor, covered seating. Finch also liked the ambiance inside, with its eclectic collection of rickety tables and old breakfast room chairs; Stache's also had two rooms that sold used books. Brasfield Finch occasionally found one of his own novels on the shelf. (He always checked the title page to see if it was inscribed to anyone; he was always amused to learn that some jerk that he knew had given away—or *sold*—his book.) Lily and Finch sat at one of the shaky, uneven tables on the porch. They were waited on by a boy with a ponytail named Randy, who had been in Finch's writing class; several of the boys and girls who worked there had been Finch's students at one time or another. They were of the Bohemian faction on campus. He referred to them as his "little crippled chickens."

Stache's, with a student sculpture over the front door of a huge, black handle-bar mustache—hence the name—was on Main Street in Lakewood. Lakewood was a village, little more than a hamlet; Main Street consisted of three blocks of shops, stores, and cafes, with a couple more bars, notably The Falcon's Nest, which catered to fraternity and sorority types, and Lucky's, an old fashioned grocery store which called itself a supermarket, but wasn't. Main Street was two blocks from the campus. The town's population was three thousand, doubling to six thousand when the college was in session.

"How is the play coming?" Finch asked her when they had their cocktails.

"Fine," she said. "I'm enjoying it."

"How's old J. J. as a director?"

"Okay, I guess," she answered. "Showy. He prances a lot. He told us he'd once played Jesus in *Jesus Christ Superstar* and I don't think he ever got over it."

"Jesus Christ!" Finch exclaimed. "Pun intended."

"I haven't been in many plays, but I think he must be pretty peculiar," she went on. "He snaps his fingers rapidly—and loudly— when he wants us to speed up the pace. 'Really, Lily?' he keeps saying to me, over and over again. He said he was pushing me because I would carry the play."

"And how is old Norman Lawrence doing? My god, he must be three days older than God!"

"Well, there seems to be some tension between him and J. J. For one thing, Norman can't remember his lines. The prompters were having to give every one of them to him, so they wrote out his speeches and taped them everywhere on the set, on the back of a lamp shade, on a book on a table, the back of a chair, just about every place Dr. Rank would be during scenes. J. J. has lost his patience with him a couple of times, and several times Norm has questioned his direction. 'Don't criticize me, Norm!' J. J. screamed one night. 'I'm not criticizing you, J. J.,' Norm said, 'I'm *helping* you!' 'Well, thanks but no thanks, you old fart!' J. J. said, much to the amusement of the cast and crew. Sometimes it's been something of a circus, but all in all the play is shaping up."

"Good. You're having fun. That's all that really matters."

"I suppose so, Brass," she said, "but I want to do a good job."

"You will, Lily, I have no doubt," he said.

"I'm limiting myself to one drink so I'll be alert at rehearsal tonight."

"My, you *are* dedicated, my dear."

They sipped their drinks. "So tell me what's been going on around campus," she said. "I've been so busy with the play and with papers and preparations—I could choke every member of the sophomore committee for changing textbooks on me after just one year— that I haven't been keeping up."

"Oh, it's been quiet, in contrast to last year. I must say I miss the ripened, naked bodies of the streaking craze." He chuckled. "There *is* a rumor going around that our corpulent dean is mounting an underground campaign for the presidency."

"Stegall is stepping down?"

"Not that I know of. But that minor detail does not seem to bother Dean Jefferson. He is a pluperfect jerk-off. But I don't imagine he could be any worse than Stegall. I'm not really sure what the fat man has in mind, though."

"It would be hard to tell with Wally."

"Wally?"

"That's what he told me to call him last year, when he was trying to get into my panties."

Finch laughed. They both had a good laugh together, and they noticed that they were attracting the stares of other patrons on the porch. So Finch said, in a lower voice,

"Did you know that son-of-a-bitch is a Klansman?"

"A *Klansman*?"

"Well, he was head of the White Citizen's Council in this county. Same thing. They are the branch of the KKK that wears ties."

"I *didn't* know that. But it figures," she said.

"Understandable when you realize he is originally from a hick town called Berry, Alabama."

"Now, Brass," she said, smiling, "you forget that I, too, am from rural Alabama."

"No, my dear. Like Aphrodite, you were born on the waves," he said.

"You really know how to please a girl, Brass," she said.

"So I've been told. On more than one occasion."

"I don't doubt it."

Finch clucked his tongue. "This place!" he said. "Stegall, Jefferson, Hoss Murphy…Russo! All the shit. *In spite* of all the shit we have to put up with, dear Lily, it's still a good life. Isn't it?"

"Yes, Brass, it is," she said.

CHAPTER SEVEN

Lily and Willow were lying naked under the rich, coffee colored duvet on Willow's double bed. Both women were quiet, resting after a bout of satisfying lovemaking, staring up at the high ceiling of Willow's bedroom with its faint ancient water stains.

"This is a wonderful old house," Lily said.

"Yes," Willow said, "I *love* Bostony House. It's one of the oldest buildings in the town of Lakewood. One of Lakewood's founders, actually, lived here, Richard Phillips Bostony. He was a state senator, and he is responsible for our college being situated here. It was at its beginning called Florida Girls' Industrial School, did you know that? This is a well-built old house."

"Yeah, I read about that," Lily said. "Look at that crown molding. It looks hand carved."

"It is," Willow said. She sighed and relaxed back into the pillows. After a few minutes she said, "I suppose you're looking forward to having Dr. Stewart here as a Yancey Lecturer."

"Well, I haven't given it much thought, lately. I've been so busy with the play and all. But yes, I'm thrilled. 'Love has pitched its tent / In the place of excrement.'"

"What's that?"

"Lines from Yeats. *The Crazy Jane Poems*."

"Oh, yes, of course. I've always been partial to others of his poems. 'I will arise and go there/ And go to Innisfree/ And a small cabin build there/ Of clay and wattles made.' And 'The golden apples of the sun/ the silver apples of the moon.'"

"Oh, wonderful, Willow! You like 'The Song of Wandering Aengus,' too. It's one of my very favorites."

"I've never taught Yeats," Willow said. "He isn't really considered a Victorian."

"Yeah. More modern. But yes, yes. I'm very excited to have Charles Stewart. Brass knows him. I think he wants to hook Dr. Stewart and me up."

"Oh, really?" Willow said. After a minute she said, "Of course you should have a younger person, Lily. You don't really know this man, but I suppose if you must have a man, then you should go for it. You don't need to spend your time with an old person like me."

"You're not *old*, Willow! And that's almost the same thing Brass said to me."

"Brasfield Finch?" Willow said. Lily was not looking at her, but she sensed the older woman tensing up.

"Yes," she said.

"Oh, my, you mean…"

"Yes."

"Good God!"

"Willow, I…"

"Just give me a minute, Lily. It'll take me a few deep breaths and a little time to get over learning that that man's *penis* has been where my mouth has been."

"Willow, I've never been anything but honest with you," Lily said. "You knew I liked men. For sex, I mean. I don't like them much otherwise."

"But Brasfield Finch?!"

"He's my friend, Willow. With benefits. Just like you."

"I thought I was more than a friend," Willow said.

"You *are,* of course. You and Brass are my very best friends *forever*!"

"You are such a child, Lily. Such a brilliant young woman, but also a child. I forget."

"It's the 'child in me.'" She laughed to diffuse the tension. They lay for a while without speaking.

"Lily, dear," Willow said, after a long pause, "you have taught me so much—about my body, about pleasure—that I am quite grateful to you. I never knew…" she trailed off.

"You told me you had had other lesbian experiences," Lily said.

"Yes, of course. But they were just fumblings, bumblings, compared to what we've shared. I never knew it could be like this. So, thank you."

"Willow! You don't need to thank *me*. *I* thank *you*."

"I'm just an old spinster school teacher, Lily."

"You're *not*! You're not *just* anything!"

"Sometimes that's how I feel. But not with you. You make me feel *alive,* Lily. You give me something to live for other than my dusty old books, my ungrateful students, and my book on Georges Sand that I don't think I will *ever* finish." She laughed then. "*That's* what I thank you for, my dear. I would say that I love you, but that would complicate things, so I'll just say that you are very, very dear to me!"

"Thank you, Willow," Lily said. "And you are to me, too! And if it's any consolation to you, my progress on my dissertation—which you once flattered me by calling a book—is as slow as molasses in January."

Willow reached over and clasped Lily's hand in hers. The younger woman's hand was soft and warm. "Don't you worry your head about that, my darling girl. I—and I suppose this old man you call Brass—will take good care of you."

"OUR PRESIDENT IS UNSTABLE!!!!!" read the headline on the mimeographed sheet that was distributed to all faculty and staff mailboxes. "HE HAD A NERVOUS BREAKDOWN LAST SPRING, AND HE HAS NOT RECOVERED!!!!! HE IS COMPLETELY DEMENTED!!!!!" It went on, with excruciatingly abhorrent detail, to bring up all the unpalatable things that had happened the previous year, things that were *not* President John W. Stegall's fault.

"Trash!" Stegall said to his secretary Eloise Hoyle, tossing the page onto his neat, uncluttered desk. "Utter Bolshevik propaganda! I won't let them get away with it this time."

"Yes sir, you go get 'em!" she said.

"How dare they say I'm 'demented'?! How could they write such crap?! Pardon my French."

"Yes sir, they are some crazy rednecks, they are."

Eloise Hoyle was tall and lean, a full head taller than her boss, with whom she had been having a "thing" since her husband, Wesley Hoyle, the former director of buildings and grounds at the college, had one day died of a heart attack in the produce aisle of Lucky's Supermarket. Eloise—she knew the students called her 'Olive' Hoyle, and she didn't like it one bit—had a tendency to wear dark gray and black, since she considered it slimming. But she was already skinny as a rail. She had a tiny protruding belly like half a soccer ball, and she had floating ribs which stuck out further than her breasts, which resembled sunny-side-up fried eggs. She liked little navy or black jackets that covered the abnormality with her ribs. Her husband Wesley and John Stegall were the only men who had ever seen her naked, and she planned to keep it that way. Neither of them had ever even seemed to notice her deformity.

"I will fire these people and then I'll sue the hell out of them for defamation of character," he said. "Pardon my French, but when I win I can get a bigger sailboat!" His face was turning red, as was the scalp under his bristly white hair.

"Settle down, John," she said, "don't let these awful people get to you."

"How can I keep from it?" he asked. "Call that bastard Wallace Jefferson and tell him to get his ass—again, pardon my French—over here!"

"Yes sir," she said, "don't forget to pump up your chair." She hastened out to her own outer office.

Jefferson settled his massive largeness into one of Stegall's visitor's chairs. He looked around the spacious, airy office (that would soon be his!). There was a small conference table against one wall, where Stegall was fond of inviting his favorites on the faculty—those whom he considered loyal—to have lunch with him. He always, without fail, ordered from the Caf sesame chicken for two. It had become something of a joke around campus, after Lillian Lallo, last year's chairperson of the faculty senate and a professor in the business department, had revealed the habit in a meeting. "Yep, sesame chicken," one of the chosen ones would say when emerging from the front door of Woodfin Hall with a toothpick in his or her mouth. There were always howls of laughter.

Against another inner wall was a large sofa upholstered in corduroy purple and gold, the Lakewood colors. Across the room, under the large window that looked out onto the quad, was an antique pecan-wood hutch that held pictures and mementos. There was a picture of John Stegall from his swing music dance-band days, in a white dinner jacket, red bow tie, and thick, wavy blonde hair that had given way over the years to his current thinning gray threads that resembled streaks of bacon grease. He had a saxophone on a lanyard around his neck. Next to his picture was one of his wife Nelle, one of those "glamour" photographs such as those taken in some department store in Tallahassee. She had a round, chubby face and "fixed" hair that was of a faded strawberry blonde tint. The first lady had taken it upon herself to plant day lilies, many, many day lilies, all around Flower Hill and all over the town of Lakewood, so there was not a vacant lot or an unoccupied patch of ground in the entire town that wasn't profusely planted with day lilies. The day lilies were to be her legacy. Since one could not kill a day lily with a stick, they would be there, in one form or another, forever, though in future years they would come to resemble weeds.

Jefferson perused the other mementos on the hutch. There was an old worn baseball glove (don't ask!) and an autographed baseball on a little stand: Mickey Mantle. There was a picture of the governor, Wayne Flintrock, signed "To John, with great respect." There was another with Stegall posing with the professional tennis player Billie Jean King, both in tennis whites, holding rackets. Jefferson had been tempted several times in the past to ask Stegall if he actually played a match with King. And who won? But he had not asked, because he didn't want to embarrass the president. Until now.

"Is that a real Mantle autograph?" he asked.

"Pardon?"

"On that baseball, John. There. Are you sure it's authentic?"

"Of course it's authentic," the president said.

"Did you get it yourself? In Yankee Stadium? The day Mantle hit his last home run? Or what?" Jefferson could barely contain the sarcasm in his voice.

"No. For your information, I ordered it from an ad in *Outdoor Life* magazine. Why, do you want one?"

"You got ripped off, John. Did you get some phony 'Statement of Authenticity' or something? It's not real."

"How the hell do you know? Mind your own business," Stegall said, beginning to slightly flush.

"And that picture of you and Billie Jean? Is that real, too? And by the way, who won the match that day? If there really was one."

"None of your business!" Stegall spat. "What is this, Wallace?"

"I've been reading about these new digital cameras, where they can superimpose any figure into any other picture. Is that really Billie Jean?"

"That's an *old* picture!"

"They can do it with old ones, too, I'm told."

Stegall's face was turning a bright red. His breathing had quickened. "I'll have you know that Billie Jean King is one of my dearest friends!" he sputtered.

"Huh," Jefferson said.

"I don't believe this!" Stegall said. "What the hell are you up to, Wallace?! Pardon my…"

"French!" the dean finished for him. "I'm not up to anything, John. I'm just worried about your welfare, that's all."

"My 'welfare?'"

"Your mental state."

"Wait a minute! You're not buying into this ignorant business in that propaganda sheet, are you, because…?" He trailed off. He took a deep breath. His face and scalp were now crimson.

"What 'propaganda sheet'?" Jefferson said calmly. "You're not referring to all that distasteful business of last year, are you?"

"No! The one that came this morning! That's why I summoned you over!"

"I haven't seen anything like that," the dean said.

"How could you miss it? Look!" Stegall pointed at his desk. It was neat and empty. The broadside was gone. "It was there just a minute ago!" he said. "Damn it to hell. Par…Par…"

"Quit apologizing for your French, John. It's not really French, anyway. And, as a dean, I've heard much worse. It's a wonder I've got any butt left, as often as I've had it chewed off in extremely choice words." He looked quizzically at the diminutive president, perched behind his mastodon of a desk on his elevated chair. "John, my friend, do you think you might have imagined it?"

"No, goddammit, I didn't imagine it! I held it in my hand! Right here!"

"I think you need to see somebody, John," the dean said.

"What did you say?" the president said shakily. "Get out of my office!"

"John…" the dean said.

"I said GET OUT OF MY OFFICE," Stegall screamed. He was now standing behind his desk.

Mrs. Hoyle stuck her head in the door. "What's going on?" she asked.

"Eloise, John is…upset," Wallace said, standing up.

"Well, I'll take care of it," she said, coming into the office.

"I said get out!" Stegall said, in a whisper.

Jefferson hastily exited the president's office with the broadside folded neatly into the side pocket of his blue serge suit jacket. He was smiling to himself.

Eloise came on in and eased John Stegall back into his chair. She sat on the arm and cradled the man's head on her shoulder. "Now,

now," she whispered, "you just calm down, my love."

"He's one of them," the president gasped.

"Who? Dean Jefferson? Oh no, dear." She patted his head gently. "He's on *our* side, John. Just take a deep breath. Remember your heart. Do your breathing that the nurse taught you. 'Smell the roses, and blow out the candles.'" She breathed with him. He obediently did his breathing. Then,

"No," he said, "he's not."

Finch was not really watching the morning local news, but a name caught his ear. He turned it up. "Rudolph Cowan, the Lakewood killer, is being released from a state mental hospital where he has been incarcerated for twenty years. Cowan murdered a coed in a ritual killing that attracted news media from around the world. He has served his time and will be released next week. In other news…" Finch turned the television down. Rudolph Cowan! God, he hadn't thought of him in years. He recalled the young man vividly; he had been in Finch's writing class when it all happened. Cowan had strangled a girl out in the woods beyond the tennis courts; he had arranged candles and flowers all around her naked body. It was days before they found the missing girl, and by then Rudolph had gone whacko, going up and down the streets of Lakewood banging on front doors and screaming that he wanted Boo Bradley, the reclusive character in Lenora Hart's *To Lynch a Wild Duck*, to come out. It didn't take the police long to connect the boy to the murdered girl; Finch shuddered, remembering the insane young man screaming vows of revenge on all of Lakewood when they took him away. Though Brasfield's memory of the trial was not completely clear, he thought Cowan had pleaded not guilty by reason of insanity; the jury had found him guilty of murder in the second degree. The judge had remanded him to the state mental hospital in Tallahassee to serve his sentence. And now he was going to be free. Not good for anybody.

Finch ran into Willow Behn in the hallway as she was going to her office. "Did you hear about Rudolph Cowan?" he asked her.

"Who?"

"Surely you remember. The young man who murdered a young girl on campus about twenty years ago."

"Twenty years ago? I had just come on board then, but, yes, I remember it. Dreadful stuff."

"He's being released."

"Released? From where?"

"From the state mental hospital. Where he served his term. He's getting out next week."

"Oh, dear," Willow said, "who told you this?"

"I heard it on the morning news."

"Those awful cheery coffee club people?"

"No," he said, "another channel."

"If I remember correctly, the boy—I suppose the man, now—promised a degree of revenge on all things Lakewood. You don't think he would do anything, do you? Surely the mental health people have improved his outlook."

"I wouldn't count on it," Finch said. "I mean the mental health people. I don't think they've ever changed *anybody's* outlook."

"Mr. Finch, you are a cynic!" She smiled.

"I wouldn't be surprised if the boy—the *man*—showed up on campus, though. He is still probably as crazy as a Betsy bug."

"The use of that word 'crazy' is not really politically correct, Mr. Finch."

"Do you think I give a flying fuck?"

She narrowed her eyes and peered at him.

After a minute, she said, "You are incorrigible!"

"So I've been told," he said.

He turned toward his door.

"Mr. Finch," she said, stopping him. "It seems that I recall this Rudolph Cowan was one of your students. Is that right?"

"Correct," he said.

They went on into their respective offices and closed their doors.

CHAPTER EIGHT

"So tell me about this guy," Lily said to Willow. They were sitting in Willow's office overlooking the quad. A gentle winter breeze drifted through the open windows.

"Not much to tell, other than what was in the papers. He killed her and scattered flowers and put burning candles around her body. Out in those woods beyond the tennis courts. Nobody ever knew why he did it. I surely don't. It's interesting that he was one of your Mr. Finch's students."

"*My* Mr. Finch?! Come on, Willow."

"Okay. You're right. I mustn't put down my rivals."

"He's not your *rival*, Willow. We fooled around once, last year. That was all." Lily suddenly recollected their recent flirting, what Brass had said. She felt herself blushing.

"The look on your face, Lily dear," Willow said, "the look on your face."

"I've never been anything more than honest with you, Willow. I..."

Willow stopped her. "Please dear. I was just—as the students say—messing with you. It's too early in the morning for a serious discussion. What does your day look like?"

"Oh, the usual. Two classes, a load of papers. And a student government advisory committee meeting. Why do they load down junior faculty with so many committees?"

"Because you are junior faculty. Next question?"

Lily laughed. "I don't have any other questions."

"Anyway, this Rudolph character was carried away screaming that he would get revenge on Lakewood," Willow went on. "As if we were responsible for his deeds. It gives one pause. Hopefully, they have straightened him out—he served his time in the state mental hospital—and we will never hear from nor see him again. But, as I say, it gives one pause."

"That was twenty years ago, Willow. He's probably forgotten all about his threats."

"Perhaps you're right, dear. I hope you are. Anyway, I think we should all keep our eyes and ears open."

"Yes. Okay. Good advice."

"That's enough of that. How's the play coming?"

"I think it's shaping up well. Opening night is Thursday. I'm a little nervous. Mr. Lawrence still doesn't know his lines. He has his own prompter in the wings, and they've taped up his lines everywhere onstage. They even put poster paper up inside the proscenium and wrote with bold black magic marker, in big letters. He refuses to wear his glasses. Even though J. J. insisted to him that Dr. Rank might well have worn spectacles."

"Pity," Willow said, shaking her head. "Vanity, thy name is male actor!"

"Even with all the lines posted everywhere, he *still* reads the wrong lines in the wrong places, making the scene he's in not make any sense. He doesn't seem to even notice."

"He probably doesn't. He's nearing the end of a hard drinking life. I'm surprised he has any brain cells left. Norman Lawrence, in his prime—or perhaps, I should say, in his depths—would have made your Mr. Finch look like an amateur."

"There you go again," Lily said, with a pout.

"I'm truly sorry, darling. Does your Mr. Lawrence—see, it was only a figure of speech—show up for rehearsals drunk?"

"Maybe that's his problem, I don't know. He seems to be somewhat unsteady on his feet. I thought that was just old age."

"Let's hope it is. Thursday night opening. I'm excited. I've reserved my ticket."

"Oh no. Call and cancel it. They gave each cast member two comps. They even let us pick where the seats are. I guess it's for parents. My parents wouldn't know what to do at a play, and they would never drive all this way even if I invited them. They never even go to movies, just watch them sometimes on television, and then it's those schmaltzy movies on The Hallmark Channel. They wouldn't understand the first thing about *A Doll's House*."

"Where is my comp seat, Lily?" She looked shrewdly at the younger woman. "And who are you giving the other seat to? I hope, dear, that they aren't together."

"No. I wanted y'all on third row center. The first two rows are too low. You are on third row left, an aisle seat, and his is third row right. Also an aisle seat. So there's a whole row between you."

"Thank you for that. I'm becoming a little fonder of Mr. Finch, but I'm not quite there yet."

"I understand, Willow."

"Has J. J. Underwood controlled himself, I mean toward you? I remember you told me about that episode last year."

"Yes, he has. I think they were just trying to get a threesome going. He seems too perverted to be turned on by straight sex."

Willow laughed heartily. "I can't imagine anyone not being turned on by sex with you, my dear, in any way, shape or form." The two women chuckled together.

Their friendly relationship had grown steadily over the year and a half Lily had been at Lakewood. It was taking Willow a while to get used to Lily's "friends with benefits" philosophy; it was not something that was remotely a part of Willow's experience. But she admired the younger woman's sense of self-direction, her confidence in who she was.

Her own parents had been stern, Victorian types, her father an attorney at a large firm in Nashville who was never at home, and her mother a matron who was involved in several book and civic and bridge clubs; they lived in Belle Mead, and her mother played bridge with the woman who played Minnie Pearl on The Grand Ole Opry, who was another Belle Mead matron. Her mother would never tell Willow the woman's real name.

"I must protect her privacy," her mother told Willow. "Her Minnie Pearl fans would not leave her alone."

"I'm not a Minnie Pearl fan," the young Willow had said. "Ugh!"

Willow was never taught anything about sex, and she grew up isolated, without many friends. She was always the tallest and smartest girl in her class, and that didn't help much. She was valedictorian of her class at Belmont Girls' Academy, and she was offered scholarships to Harvard, Yale and Princeton. But her father, an extremely conservative and opinionated man, would not let her go northeast.

"No southern woman has any business going to one of those Yankee Ivy schools," he said, putting his foot firmly down. It angered Willow, but it never occurred to her that she could defy her father and go anyway. It made her hate and distrust conservatives—her father was the president of the Middle Tennessee Republicans—and it turned her toward finding her own way.

She went to Peabody, on full scholarship, with the intention of becoming a teacher, a profession of which her father approved for a "southern woman of her class." She lived on campus, at North Hall, and she graduated with highest honors and won a Woodrow Wilson Fellowship to Vanderbilt. Her father expressed his disapproval at a woman doing graduate study, but he couldn't disapprove of Vanderbilt, a distinguished southern university and practically in their own back yard. She eventually, by the hardest persistence, earned her PhD there; many of her professors were practically carbon copies of her father, and since she was one of the first women to enter the graduate program—indeed, she became the first woman to be granted a PhD at Vandy—they made it extremely difficult for her.

Her experiences with her father and her professors had toughened her and, she feared, hardened her. But she was who she was. She maneuvered the English department at Lakewood with ease. Eleanor Buffkin and Katharine Klinger, two older women—they were holdovers from when the school was an all-girls college—

who taught American Literature and Chaucer, were easy to get along with, though Willow, who was not *that* far behind them in age, thought of them as another generation. Eleanor was of middle height, with blonde hair (surely dyed) and was thin and wiry. She had a sharp tongue that intimidated the younger instructors. (Not Lily, Willow was sure.) Katharine Klinger was short and plump, with a round face and gray hair put up in a bun at the back of her head; she wore little knitted bands over her head that were tied with a bow beneath her chin. She referred to them as "her fascinators." She wore roomy skirts down almost to her ankles and comfortable shoes, sometimes sneakers. The students called her "The Chaucer Lady."

But Katharine was not, in Willow's estimation, the most eccentric member of the department. That distinction belonged to their chairman, Rufus Doublet, who, even though he was from a little hamlet in Georgia, little more than a cross-roads, called Lickskillet, pronounced his name "Doo-blay," as though it were French. He was in his forties and was what Willow called a "professional southerner;" he spoke with an exaggerated drawl that he obviously thought was cute but came out as extremely effeminate. He was a good looking man, and he knew it; he had dark, curly hair and a ruddy, tanned Florida complexion. He wore a series of very nice tweed sports jackets paired with appropriate Dockers, button down collars and narrow knit ties. He was excessively unctuous, and Willow could not stand him, and neither, from what she could gather, could Lily, though the younger woman was hesitant to say too much about him since she was a junior faculty member without tenure. Willow sensed that something unpleasant had passed between the two, but Lily would not talk about it. Willow could readily guess what it might have been! The man had at times even seemed to be, as the students say, "coming on" to *her*, which Willow found hard to believe and dismissed as silly, but she knew, from past experience, that Rufus Doublet had a proclivity for older women. *Much* older women. Willow had even wondered if Doublet had ever "come on" to Eleanor and Katharine, but she wouldn't dare ask them.

Finch was sitting at his desk opening his mail. His windows were flung open to the day, which was lovely; the grinning meteorologist on the morning news had said the high would be 73 degrees. Much of Finch's mail was disposable. He tossed the red hand-mail envelopes, usually from administrators or people making announcements of events that Finch cared nothing about, in the trash can without opening them. Likewise the stack of books, still in their mailers, that had been sent to him for his "inspection and consideration." Finch used no textbook in his writing classes; most of these complimentary books were freshman English texts or sophomore survey anthologies. In Finch's opinion, publishers must spend a fortune sending out books to people who will never even look at them, much less consider them. Finch imagined that some of his colleagues probably eagerly opened and perused every book that came in the mail. He thought that was a waste of time and did not respect those few who might have done it.

He was surprised to find a personal letter in the stack; it was in a long, white business envelope with the return address of his old friend, and former lover, Cassandra Birmingham. She was a novelist, and a very successful one. He himself would never want fame or any sort of celebrity status such as that enjoyed by Lenora Hart, the super famous author of the putrid *To Lynch a Wild Duck*, a children's story that had crossed over into adult fiction and become, over the years since its publication, one of the most beloved books of the American people. (Which, Finch thought, said as much about the American people as it did about the novel.) Still, Finch did envy Cassandra's ascendancy in the literary world. He even envied her prosperity. He was not money hungry, but he would have enjoyed being able to pick up and go off to Europe for a couple of months any time he wanted. Cassandra commanded advances in the low-mid six figures; he knew this because a former agent of his, Al Bernstein (who had also been Cassandra's agent at one time, before she bolted for a larger and more prestigious agency) kept him informed. Al Bernstein could have been a character right out of *Guys and Dolls*, even to the cigar. He had nagged Finch to be more commercial. "You need to write a blockbuster!" he would say. But Finch didn't *want* to write blockbuster; he wanted to write what he wanted to write. They finally had a big falling out over it. Finch had heard on the grapevine that Al had landed the famous British novelist Ken Buckalaney, who sold zillions of copies of his novels, which appeared with impressive regularity every three years and, when they appeared in paperback, packed the mass market stands in every airport in the world. Al finally had his blockbuster. Finch hoped he was happy.

The letter from Cassandra was a chatty one, asking about his health and well-being. She was undoubtedly the most attractive woman (before Lily, of course) that he had ever slept with. Her book-jacket photos were stunning; she was a slim and trim woman who, Finch was sure, would have no need of a face-lift, though she could well afford one, or two or three, if she desired. She had had (and probably—likely—still did) the most beautiful ass he'd ever seen on a woman. Maybe even better than Lily's, though she didn't have Lily's fleshy curves and her gorgeous and stunning breasts, which were just the right size, not too large, and delicious, he might add. Finch was turned off by women who had overlarge, buxom breasts; he thought they looked deformed.

Finch had read in *The New York Times Book Review* that Cassandra Birmingham's new novel was about to be published. It was set in Highlands, North Carolina, and was entitled *Moonshine*. She was probably in the half-million range now. She lived on the Outer Banks in North Carolina. And here he was in Lakewood, in the sandy scrub of the Florida Panhandle; but it was *his* choice. And he was glad he had made it. His was, after all, a good life.

He sat looking out his window at the perfect day, fanaticizing about Cassandra's splendid, alluring and concupiscent ass. He was startled out of his reverie by the ringing of his phone. It was Alicia Martin, the dean's secretary, summoning him to a meeting with the dean that afternoon. *Oh shit*, he thought, *what have I done now?*

"Brasfield," Dean Jefferson said—(Using his first name; not a good sign, he usually called him Mr. Finch. Or maybe it *was* a good sign; perhaps the dean wanted something.) "—it's been a while. How have you been?"

"Just fine, thank you," said Finch.

The dean settled himself back into his desk chair; it creaked under his bulk, as if it were complaining. He smiled at Finch. Jefferson usually didn't smile at anything. *Uh-O*, thought Finch.

"Brasfield," he said (using the first name again, in a cozy good old boy way), "just what do you think of President Stegall?"

"What do you mean, what do I think of the son-of-a-bitch?" Finch asked.

"Not much love lost there, huh?"

"Not love, Wallace, that's what goes on between the sheets. Or have you forgotten all about that? No, you haven't. I heard you've been banging your secretary."

"Who told you that?!" the dean said huffily. "How dare you..." Then he seemed to catch himself. He smiled again. He leaned forward and whispered, "It's all the same, Brasfield. Pussy, I mean."

"Vulgarity is not your forte, Dean Jefferson. You say that word as if you've never said it before."

"What word?"

"Pussy."

"Oh, yes, I remember an unpleasant conference last year with you and some irate parents about that word. It seemed that you had referred to the young lady's pussy in class. You talked about kissing it, wasn't that it?"

"I was talking about a cat in a story she wrote."

"Oh yes, I remember now. That's how we settled it. Though

I must tell you that I don't think the parents were pleased with the result. He was a Baptist preacher, you know."

"What did you ask me in here about, Wallace? I really have some manuscripts to read and a class to prepare for." Neither of which was true.

"Oh yes." The smarmy smile again. "I asked you what you thought of our president. I was wondering if you had noticed anything about his mental state."

"His mental state? I rarely see the man, Wallace, and when I do I hardly notice him. He's such a flake."

"Yes, that's exactly what I hoped you had noticed. His flakiness. I'm worried about him, Brasfield. I think he is on the verge of a breakdown."

"I think he's been on the verge for ages," Finch said.

"Well, a group of concerned faculty members have come to me—I am not at liberty to tell you who they are" (Finch could well imagine who they were)—"and asked me about what might happen if the man...well, becomes incapacitated midstream, right in the middle of the academic year."

"What do you mean, Wallace? The board would appoint an interim president, and we'll begin the tedious search for a new head to wear the crown. Please promise me that if anything like that should happen, you won't put me on the dreaded search committee."

"Done. I promise." Jefferson actually crossed the heart beneath the lapel of his blue serge suit. If such a thing as a heart veritably existed in the chests of administrators; Finch had serious doubts about that. "The thing is: the group has invited me to meet with them. And they would like to get as many faculty as they can to join their group. As a senior faculty member, Brasfield, I'm asking you if you'd like to accompany me to a group meeting."

"I don't do groups, Wallace. It's against my nature to *join* anything."

"I'm well aware of your preferences, Brasfield, but in this case..."

"No," Finch said. "Period."

"Well, perhaps you'll think about it and decide to join us," the dean said.

"I doubt it, on both counts," Finch said. "Is that all you wanted to talk to me about today? I really must…" He made motions to stand.

"Of course," the dean said. "You're a busy man, I know. Yes, that was all I wanted. I'll bet you thought another one of your students had complained about you, about you drinking and coming to class." He was still smiling the fulsome, oleaginous smile. "No, no, no, nothing of that this time," he said. "My friend, you seem to be keeping your nose clean."

His friend? "I don't know about that, Wallace," he said, standing, "but I *am* a busy man." Finch's jeans, boots and wrinkled denim work shirt contrasted sharply with the dean's freshly cleaned and pressed suit. Finch wondered if the dean's suit was a XXXL size, or if they even made suits that large. He supposed that's what they sold in those "big and tall" stores he saw advertised on television. But, *Ah yes*, he thought, *Dean Wallace Jefferson probably has his suits tailor-made, as did, surely, President John W. Stegall III. Except that Stegall could easily buy his from the junior boy's section of the Sears-Roebuck catalogue.*

"It was nice to talk with you, Brasfield," the dean said. He seemed to be struggling to get out of his chair and stand.

"Don't get up, Wallace," Finch said, "I can show myself out. And likewise, about the talk I mean."

When he went through the outer office Alicia Martin glared at him. *Such a pleasant world over here in administrative land*, Finch thought wryly. *That bastard is up to something, and I believe I know what it is. I think he has me confused with someone who gives a shit.*

CHAPTER NINE

Lily was so nervous her heart was beating in her throat. The younger girls in the dressing room—the props girls and the girl playing Emma—were yakking and giggling. (There were only two dressing rooms backstage, one for men and one for women.) Lil Magill was sitting calmly in a corner smoking a cigarette, despite the fact that J. J. Underwood had asked her not to smoke anywhere inside the theater. She told Lily that she didn't give a good goddamn what J. J. said. (Lily had once heard Lil Magill say to J. J. Underwood, referring to the tiny girl who was playing Nora's daughter, "If you let that little shit upstage me I'll whack you and her both over the head!") Lil was a fairly good actress, though she played Mrs. Lende with a few histrionics that Lily didn't think were appropriate for the part; Underwood seemed to like them. Both Underwoods liked exaggerated gestures; Tulah had strutted around the stage in one of Mrs. Linde's costume dresses. "*Wear* your costume," she had said dramatically, "*Live in* your costume. Let your costume become you!" She flounced the skirt of the dress around energetically as she marched around the stage in front of the cast. Lily could see no place in the play where such a gesticulation was called for, but she had kept her mouth shut.

Lily was wearing a yellow dress that buttoned demurely at the throat. She would wear a similar one—blue—in the second act until she changed into her new "party dress." Those would be her three costumes until she changed into her "traveling clothes," as J. J. called them, at the end of the play; her "traveling clothes" consisted of a severe black suit and heavy shoes, which Lily found difficult to walk in. She did not think her closing costume was suitable for a newly liberated woman; it seemed more funereal than free. But, again, Lily kept her mouth shut. What did she know?

Lucas Haas, the stage manager, stuck his head in the door. Without knocking. Lil had put out her cigarette and was preparing to don her costume. She was standing in front of the mirror in only her panties and bra. The stage manager's face announced that that was exactly what he had hoped to see by barging in; he glanced over at Lily, who had been fully costumed and made up for half an hour. His disappointment was apparent. Lil barked in her cigarette- and (Lily suspected) whiskey-deep voice, "Take a good look, you little shit, because that's as close as you'll ever come to this juicy!"

"Five minutes," Lucas Haas said. He ducked his head back out the door.

Lily felt her stomach fluttering. "Do you think I should go on out in the wings?" she asked Lil Magill. The little student playing Emma was sitting against the wall in her costume dress, her feet stretched out in front of her. She seemed to be asleep.

"Go on," Lil said, "I'm not on for a while. Big Eyes will come get me when it's time for my cue."

Lily went out into the backstage dimness. There was much last minute bustle going on, the props people checking the set, the stage manager yelling at the lights people in the booth at the back of the theater through his headphone. "Too much light on the curtain!" Lucas said in a stage yell, "dim it!"

J. J. Underwood was peeking out through a crack in the curtain. He turned around and looked at Nora in her yellow dress and Torvald in his frock coat and vest, which did not seem to Lily quite appropriate for a man working at home, but then, again, what did she know?

"Full house," he said. "They're yakking it up, so they're excited. It'll be a good audience for you two, my stars. So give it your all! Break a leg!" He disappeared back into the dimness. Lily took her spot, the exact place she'd been in for dress rehearsal. She thought about Willow and Brass, sitting out there in their respectively separated seats. She swallowed and cleared her throat. She was running lines in her head. They were sprinting through her brain like a teletype. She hoped her hands were not shaking. She hoped she would not sweat under her arms and stain the yellow dress.

"Don't do that," Max Tingle said to her.

"What?" she said.

"Run your lines in your head. It's too late for that; it'll only make you nervous. You've got to live them now."

"Live them?"

"Yes, Lily. You are doing a great job. On that stage you *are* Nora. You *become* this woman. When you make your entrance before this big audience you'll have a momentary freak-out; just swallow and forge beyond it. Relax and *be* her. Then you'll be this woman in 1879, in this stuffy Victorian drawing room, you'll feel the suffocation in the Helmer household, you will actually *become* Nora. I have confidence in you, dear."

Then she felt his hand on her ass. An aggressive butt grab; his fingers went into her crack.

"Not now, Max," she whispered irritably, "not fucking now!"

He removed his hand. "Okay," he said. "Sorry. Inappropriate time, inappropriate place."

Lily could see the girl playing the maid waiting in the other wing. Jimmy Vickery, playing the porter, came up behind them with the scraggly Christmas tree.

"Shit," Max said, "I told J. J. last night to get a better tree."

"This is it," Jimmy Vickery said.

"That's the *better* one?"

"No, it's the same one."

"Shit," Max said.

Lily didn't care what the tree looked like. It was only onstage for a few minutes anyway. She just hoped it wouldn't get a laugh and throw her off. But she would be ready if it did. She *was* ready for her entrance. *Let's go, let's go*, she was thinking. Lily chewed her lip and then stopped herself. She didn't want to mess up her makeup, which the make-up girl had literally *caked* on.

"Let's get this party started," she said to the two men.

"Yes, let's," Max Tingle said. His makeup was just as thick; with his lipstick and long hair he looked almost in drag. She hoped *that* didn't get a laugh. She thought, *How* will *I cope with unexpected laughter?* J. J. had told them that audiences often laughed in in-apropos places, and warned them not to be startled by them.

When the curtain went up and the lights came up on the empty set, the audience shushed. Lily felt her stomach grip. *Oh my god, why did I let myself get into this?* she thought. She saw Lucas counting the seconds. (J. J. had told them that the stage must remain empty for a few long seconds, because the audience would be anticipating an *entrance,* and that entrance would be Nora's. "A lesser playwright would have put the maid on the stage dusting or something when the lights come up, but not our old boy Hank Ibsen," J. J. had said. "He wants the audience to see Nora first!" *Why the hell did he have her ring the bell to her own house then*? Lily had wondered. Maybe because she had all these packages, which one of the props girls had just handed her, as light and empty as they were.

She heard the ringing of the doorbell beside her; the outer door scraped open. (J. J. had wanted the door to be noisy; he had had the guys who built the set make the door and its frame extra strong and sturdy, "so she can bang the hell out of it at the end!" he had said. "Even if it's off-stage, we don't want the fucking thing tipping over!")

The stage manager pointed to her and a stage hand, giving them her cue. "Break a leg," he whispered. Lily hoped she really would break her leg and get out of this. She made her entrance; the lights were so bright she wanted to squint. They seemed brighter than they'd been at dress rehearsal; in spite of being warned not to, Lily snuck a peek at the audience. She thought she saw the silhouette of Brass, sitting upright on the aisle. ("*Whatever* you do, don't ever, ever make eye contact with someone in the audience; it will shock you out of your stage world and into theirs! The audience is not there. Ignore them. That darkness is the fourth wall of the set. Remember that! It's a *blank* wall!")

When Lily entered, there was scattered feeble applause. *Is that a joke on me?* she wondered briefly, *or are they just glad the play has finally started?* (J. J. had held the curtain until almost fifteen minutes after eight, when the play was supposed to start at eight.) She took a deep breath. Her butterflies were slightly subsiding. She turned carefully to her right, upstage. ("Never turn your back on the audience!" Underwood had said. *Then I'm not ignoring them, I'm remembering them!* She thought.) She turned to the porter. He was still off-stage, grinning at her; Jimmy Vickery was a student in her sophomore English class. Her mind went blank. He was not in the audience, but she *knew* him. *My God*, she thought, *is it going to be like this with every-Goddam-body in the play?*

The porter stepped through the door behind her, holding the Christmas tree. She thought she heard titters at its scragglyness. *Goddammit, I can't remember my first line!*

"How much," Nora said, without Lily even thinking.

That's it! Don't think. Just be Nora!

"Fifty ore," the porter said.

Nora fumbled in her purse and came out with a coin. (It was actually a Susan B. Anthony silver dollar.)

"Here's a crown. No, keep the change," Nora said. (J. J. had informed them that she was giving him a 100 ore coin, about six-pence; there are 100 ore in a crown or krone, which is worth thirteen-pence, half penny. Thus she was tipping him a hundred percent; J. J. said that this was to establish right off the bat what a spendthrift she was. Lily doubted that anyone in the audience, except maybe Willow Behn or Brasfield Finch, even knew what a crown was or would care if they did. But, again, what did she know? Surely the people in Ibsen's time knew. And, she supposed, that's what counted. Besides, there was plenty of passive aggressive banter on Torvald's part in the first act and throughout the play to "establish" what he thought of Lily. And thought of all women.)

She heard the maid crossing the stage behind her. She spun around to her left, again not wanting to turn her back on the audience, and almost lost her balance.

"Take the tree, Ellen, and hide it so the children won't see it before it is dressed," she said.

"Yes mam," the maid said, and crossed back stage left with the tree. There were no titters. When the maid exited, she could see Torvald over there waiting for his first-act cue. He gave her a thumbs up and then a peace sign. She put her packages down, being careful, as her director had instructed her, to handle them as though they were heavy and not just empty boxes. She groped around among the packages and came out with a box of macaroons, one of which she popped in her mouth. It was delicious.

Nora was alone on stage. She felt calm and cool. The lights now seemed a normal drawing room brightness. She walked around the stage, feeling at home. "Ummm, ummm," she said, chewing another macaroon.

"Is that my little twitter-bird out there?" Torvald said offstage. Lily reacted as Nora. She frowned and hid the package of macaroons; she was annoyed at Torvald. She felt it as Nora. He was interrupting a moment of pleasure, the kind of little moment that came too infrequently to Nora. Lily realized that she was *acting. This is a piece of cake!*

Torvald stuck his head out of his study door. "Yes, that's my little canary bird," he said. *Canary bird?* She didn't think that was the right line. But no matter.

"Yes, Torvald, it's me," she said gaily.

And so the play was off and running.

Things went smoothly for a while in the first act. Some of Torvald's speeches seemed to her strangely convoluted, as if he were struggling through them. She listened intently, responding to him with her carefully retained lines—that seemed to come easily and naturally to her—even when his was slightly off key and he dropped her cue. *What is going on with this prick?* she thought. Then, *I can do this, I can do this.*

Later in the act, Nora gave him this line: "Have you remembered to invite Dr. Rank?"

Max Tingle did not respond. He looked at her, drops of perspiration on his forehead beginning to run his make-up; his face and eyes were completely blank, except for a look of panic. Finally he said, in a quaking voice, "Nora, I don't know what to say!"

He had forgotten his lines. Lily thought, *why don't you just say "yes," you numskull!* Her eyes narrowed. There was a long silence. She thought she heard some rustling of programs behind the fourth wall; some members of the audience were restless with the extended pause. He was looking pleadingly at her. She wondered if she should embarrass him further in pay-back for the butt grab. Then she felt sorry for him. She fed him his lines:

"I know it's not necessary, Torvald, dear. You can ask him when he looks in today."

The relief on his face was radiant. She detected the split second that he remembered the rest of his speech. "Oh yes," he said. "I've ordered some capital wine. Nora, you can't think how I look forward to this evening."

So it went until Dr. Rank made his entrance. There was tension backstage and tension *on*stage because of Norman Lawrence's inability to remember any lines. The man made a theatrical entry, leaning on his cane, his frock coat already dribbled on the front with something that Lily hoped was not whiskey. He emoted with a grand passion and an affected tone of voice. He looked every bit the part of a very sick Dr. Rank.

In spite of all the speeches taped everywhere on the set—meticulously hidden from the audience's view—Lawrence paraphrased his every speech. The old man looked inordinately proud of himself; *my God*, thought Lily, *the man thinks he is* improving *the play, rewriting Ibsen on the spot!* She had never seen such hubris in her entire life. She had to shake her head, but she did it imperceptibly because of all the eyes focused on her. *Don't think about the audience and their eyes!* When she was close to Dr. Rank for one of their exchanges, she smelled the whiskey. She didn't think she'd detected it, except occasionally, during rehearsals; for opening night, it was powerful. *The man not only can't recall his lines and, apparently, has made little effort to do so, but he is drunk!* She found herself paraphrasing her own lines, in response to his gibberish; if she had thought responding on cue with Max Tingle was difficult, this was near impossible. She was greatly relieved when Dr. Rank made his exit.

Lil Magill, as Christine Linde, was much easier to work with; she had a way of reciting her lines that was almost equal in staginess to Norman Lawrence, but at least she was sober. (Lily supposed her method was because of her opera background.) She gave her lines precisely, never mangling them, and Lily relaxed more with her, knowing that Mrs. Linde's response cues would be on the button. The two women performed well together.

And Lily did the same with the other actors in the play. She did not care for the student playing Krogstad; he sneered too much and was entirely too unpleasant, in Lily's opinion. But he was a good actor.

In the second act, in a dialogue with Torvald, Lily realized he had dropped his lines and was reciting a speech from the *third* act. It made no sense in the context. Lily nudged him back into the proper sequence for the scene. Again, Max Tingle looked grateful. *Maybe now you'll keep your fingers out of my crack,* thought Lily*, you son-of-a-bitch!*

When Dr. Rank made his second act appearance, Lily thought he looked as though he had fortified himself with more drink. When he told Nora that he was dying, he used many vocal histrionics, with overly large gestures as well, showing her the card he will leave with a black X marked on it when he is near the final hour, so she will know. He flashed the card to the audience with a flourish. He was pretty convincing; Nora thought she heard a gasp from beyond the footlights. When he professed his love for her, his breath almost knocked her over. She had no problem discouraging him, changing the subject, standing and getting her party dress to show him. With new stockings. He fingered the stockings sensually and sobbed; *My God, old man, get hold of yourself!* She didn't know if she were thinking as Nora or as Lily. From the way he was looking at her, she knew he was imagining the stockings on *Lily's* legs rather than Nora's.

When the Tarantella scene came, things got decidedly worse. Since Norman Lawrence couldn't play the piano, he was supposed to sit there, with the keyboard angled away from the audience, and pretend to play, while the men in the lighting and sound booth would play a recording of a Tarantella. Nora, in her new party dress, was poised and ready, but no sound came. (J. J. had told them that the Tarantella was a nineteenth century dance, so named because it was thought to be a cure for someone who had been bitten by a tarantula.)

In the long silence, Nora stood with her arms over her head. The two men looked at her as though she had the solution to the problem. The music did not come. She began to dance, twirling her skirt. (She thought she heard J. J.'s muffled "Goddammit to hell!" from the back of the theater.)

Torvald said, "Dance, Nora!"

Dr. Rank stood up. "Yes, dance Nora!" he said.

She did the steps she had been taught, whirling around. (She had no idea if this was the real Tarantella, or something that J. J. and Tulah had made up.)

"Dance, Nora!" Dr. Rank said again.

"Dance, Nora!" Torvald said.

They kept saying it, barking it at her, as she went faster and faster. The dance became a frenzy, with the two men shouting at her like two cowboys in a western movie; all they needed was pistols in their hands. She whirled and stomped, trying to dance the way she would if she, herself, had been bitten by a tarantula. *Did it make you go mad?!* Finally, she stopped. The two men politely clapped, as did the audience, to her great surprise. She had expected howls of laughter.

Toward the end of the third act, Ibsen had written a long monologue for Torvald, to cover while Nora went off to change out of her party costume. Max Tingle mauled it. As the props girls helped her change into her "traveling clothes," Lily could hear him out there grappling with it. The speech is filled with all sorts of ironies, since Torvald thinks Nora is changing for bed and he is going to get him some nookie. Most of the sardonicism was lost in Tingle's inane ramblings. Nora, dressed, listened in vain for her entry cue. "That motherfucker is lost in the wilderness," she whispered to the prop girls, who covered their mouths and giggled. How long should she let him go on? How long could the twit last? She smiled. Let him dangle a bit more. She was ready for her entrance and could see him out there, pacing back and forth, rewriting Ibsen. *If "Old Hank," as J. J. had called him, had written such drivel his work would have long since been consigned to that great theater in the sky.*

I'll just have to pick my spot, Lily thought. She entered right in the middle of one of his rambling, stuttering sentences. He turned to her, again with great relief on his face. She could see him getting back into Torvald.

"Nora," he said, "you've changed. But not…not for bed. What…"

"Yes, Torvald, I'm not sleeping here tonight," Nora said.

Then there followed the long, painful dialogue between the two, in which Nora tried to explain to Torvald why she was leaving. Lily and Max pulled it off without a flub. He really was a good actor, and she fed off him. *Why couldn't he always remember his lines?*

When Lily slammed the door, hard, just as J. J. had directed her to do, in spite of its sturdiness and the two stage hands holding it, it almost tipped over. Lily had wondered why J. J. didn't just let one of backstage people slam it; he wanted *her* to do it. It seemed important to him. So slam it she did.

She heard Torvald's last gasping plea, which Tingle did well, and then the lights came down. There was a second or two of silence, then loud, almost deafening applause. Lily had not expected that; she had been sure she would hear boos and catcalls. In the darkness

Tingle moved beside her and grasped her hand.

"We really knocked it out of the park!" he said.

"We did?!" Lily said.

The lights came back up. They had rehearsed the curtain call (Lily had not been at all sure there would even be one) and the porter, the nurse, the maid and the children went out first. Then Krogstad, Mrs. Linde and Dr. Rank together. She and Tingle entered the bath of bright lights; the others had left a gap in the middle for them. When they got to their spot the applause increased in volume. *Jesus H. Christ*! thought Lily. They all bowed together. Then Norman Lawrence stepped forward and went down on one knee; he grunted, and Lily could hear his bones popping even with the applause. He gave a grandiose wave of his arm, indicating Lily. "Our shtar!" he said, almost toppling forward. Lil Magill had to grab him.

Lily took a step downstage. The crew had brought up the house lights half-way and she could see the audience; she could see Brass and Willow. They were standing, applauding enthusiastically; the entire audience was doing the same. A standing ovation! *They are just being kind*, thought Lily.

Afterward, still in costume and make-up, Lily went out into the foyer of the theater, where Brass and Willow were waiting for her. Brass held a dozen long-stem red roses in the crook of his arm.

"Lily, darling," Willow said, taking her into an embrace, with a kiss on the cheek, and then stepping back. "You were *marvelous*, dear," she said, "marvelous!"

I was? "I was?" Lily said.

"Of course you were, beautiful lady," Brass said. "I've never seen a better Nora!"

"You probably never saw another Nora," Willow said.

"You'd be surprised," he said. "I saw Grace Kelly do it, on Broadway. She was good." He gave the flowers to Nora. "But not as good as our little Lily!"

"You're not serious," Lily said.

"Oh, yes I am," Finch said.

Just then Dean Wallace Jefferson came bounding up. "Lily, Lily, my lovely Lily," he emoted, giving her a bear hug. "You were superb, my dear. The play was a *huge* success, and it couldn't have been without you."

"Thank you, Dean Jefferson. But the rest of the crew and cast…"

"Oh, a bit amateurish," he whispered, leaning forward, "but you, lovely Lily, are a pro!" She had been about to give them all the credit, in spite of all the mistakes and blundering.

She felt like a real impostor. She was not a "pro." She could not have been as good as they were saying. And she thought the play had been a real bomb.

"Oh, Lily, my Nora," J. J. Underwood said coming up. "That was the best play I've ever directed. You were all fabulous! I've never had a play come off without a single hitch before, but this was one!" *Were you watching the same play I was?! If this was your best, I'd hate to see some of your other ones.*

"Thank you, J. J.," she said.

She saw Norman Lawrence's wife practically carrying him through the lobby. "We have to get ready for the cast party," he said to them.

"I thought the cast party was after the *last* performance," Lily said.

"Oh, we have one after every performance," Annette, his wife, said.

"Well," Lily said, "I'm afraid I'm too tired. I'm just going to go home and tuck onto bed." She looked at Brass and Willow. "Alone."

"Of course, dear," Willow said. "You really must be tired. But get those roses into a vase."

"I'll drive you home," Finch said.

"No thanks, Brass. That's sweet, but I'd like the walk. To clear my head."

"Certainly," Finch said.

Lily walked across the quiet campus in her street clothes, jeans and a deep purple Lakewood sweatshirt. The moon was full and the live oaks were resplendent in the silver light. *Maybe I was that good*, Lily thought. *As Jake Barnes says, at the end of* The Sun Also Rises, *"Isn't it pretty to think so?"*

CHAPTER TEN

Once again, they were sitting around in R. D. Wettermark's Auburn themed den, or his man-cave, as he called it. They were Alexander Daniels, Garcia Russo, Donald Katz, Fred C. Dobbs and Dean Wallace Jefferson. They were to be joined later by Perry Moon, of the social work division of Social Sciences. Jefferson was relaxing in one of Wettermark's plush leather recliners; there were five of them, lined up in front of the television, enough for all of the men but not R. D. He seemed happy enough to be making the drinks, pouring them strong as per the dean's instructions, since the dean had brought a half gallon of Old Hickory Bourbon. (Jefferson had left the Maker's Mark on the shelf; *no sense wasting the good stuff on these bozos*, he had thought.)

They were discussing the play. "My wife tried to make me go, but shit, when I take my tie off at night I don't want to go out to some prissy theater," Fred C. Dobbs was saying. "Besides, I heard it was some goddamn femi-nazi shit."

"It was very good," Jefferson said, "though, like you, I didn't care for the message. God forbid that Paulette would ever be a feminist!"

"Femi-*nazi!*" said Dobbs.

"I didn't go either," Donald Katz said. "With that girl from the English department in it, I figured it would be just some tits and ass show."

"You don't like tits and ass? Oh boy, don't be coming up behind me!" Garcia Russo said.

"Fuck you, you fucking wetback," Katz responded.

"What did you call me?!" Russo said.

"Gentlemen! Gentlemen," said the dean. "Playful banter is one thing, but let's not get ugly, Donald."

"What did he call me?" Russo said, to the gathering in general.

"Never mind, Garcia," Katz said, "don't get your panties in a wad!"

"Fuck *you*, Katz," said Russo. He was angry, red in the face.

"GENTLEMEN!" the dean said again. "Let's not, okay? We have important business here tonight."

"We're waiting on Perry," R. D. said.

"Well, while we're waiting," Jefferson said, settling back into the soft recliner, (*I really must get me one of these*, he thought) "I'll give you my drama review: the young lady in question was superb."

"What young lady?" Dobbs said.

"Miss Putnam. In the play. She was super!" Jefferson said.

Garcia Russo sneered at him. "You banging that, Wallace?" he growled.

"I'll never tell," the dean said with a smug smile.

"Oh, come on, Dean," R. D. said.

"Yeah!" Dobbs said.

"Tell us!" R. D. said. His tongue was practically hanging out.

"I told you, I'm not a kiss and tell kind of fellow," Jefferson said. "So you boys just settle down. We need to think. We need to brainstorm. Let's get back on task." He took a long swig of his drink and couldn't help but frown. (It was not nearly as smooth as Pappy Van Winkle, which he splurged on and didn't tell Paulette. He kept the Pappy Van Winkle in his desk drawer in his office at the college for a quick toddy before heading home to his yakking wife; sometimes he shared a drink with Alesha Martin, his secretary and sometime mistress. She giggled when she drank the expensive bourbon. He flashed back to the time last year when he had made something of a fool of himself in front of The Lovely Lily. Jefferson also kept a half-gallon of Smirnoff Vodka in his filing cabinet for pick-me-ups during the day. He was certain that nobody could smell vodka on one's breath, but he chewed tic-tacs all day as a precaution. He didn't buy any of that expensive vodka; Smirnoff was good enough for him. All vodkas were the same: fiery Russian communist stuff! Anyway, he had had a conference with Miss Putnam in his office one afternoon, and he had had two or three vodka snorts earlier, and he had impulsively offered The Lovely Lily a drink of Pappy Van Winkle, and he had joined her. The whiskey had gone straight to his head and caused him to behave in a very un-dean-like way. He winced inwardly every time he thought of the incident.) "I've been thinking, maybe we should invite a woman to join our group," the dean said.

"A woman?" Dobbs said. "Fuck no!"

"Maybe that Putnam girl? That what you got in mind, Dean-o?" asked R. D. Wettermark.

Just then the doorbell rang.

"That must be Perry Moon," R. D. said, "I'll go let him in."

"Let your wife answer it, R. D.," Dobbs said.

"She's not here," R. D. said as he was leaving the den to go up the hall, "she's at garden club."

"Oh, hell, that's right," said Russo. "Libby's there, too. Women!" he said, apropos of nothing.

"No, no, no, no, I wasn't thinking of Lily Putnam," Jefferson said.

"You get a hard-on when you *do* think of her, don't you Dean?!" Dobbs said, and all the men laughed jovially.

"If you can still get a hard-on," Russo sneered.

Jefferson ignored him. The man was certainly one of the most unpleasant people he'd ever known. The dean still secretly smarted about the time Russo had called him a liar in a faculty meeting. He remembered the old saying: when you lie down with dogs, you get up with fleas. Russo had never apologized for the episode, and Jefferson did not expect him to, but Russo was handy for Jefferson to use and use him he would. "I was thinking more of some senior faculty member," the dean said.

"Who you got in mind?" Katz asked in his put-on drawl. Jefferson distrusted Katz; he was a Yankee turned fake southerner, and his wife wore hippy-like clothes: long, colorful skirts, loose blouses, usually a scarf on her head. She went around to all the flea markets and arts and crafts fairs in the area selling her jewelry that she made with stones and rocks she'd found. Jefferson couldn't imagine who might buy the stuff.

"I don't know, Donald," the dean said, "who would *you* suggest?"

"Well now, I don't know," Katz drawled, crossing his long bony legs. When not in class, he usually dressed "Florida style:" Bermuda shorts, T shirt, and sandals. "I haven't really thought about it. This is a new idea." His T shirt read "Fort Walton Beach" on the chest.

At that point, R. D. came back in with Perry Moon. Moon was a fleshy, portly young man with a round baby face that befitted his name; he had a strange little goatee or something growing below his lower lip and limp brown hair down to his shoulders. Jefferson did not whole-heartedly approve of facial hair, and he thought Perry Moon's growth to be preposterous. But from what he'd been told, Moon would be a good ally over in social sciences. He was about twenty years younger than anyone else in R. D.'s man-cave. *Maybe he'll be a firebrand*, the dean thought.

"Good evening, Perry, how are you?" Jefferson said. Out of the corner of his eye he could see Russo shifting stiffly in his chair. Jefferson had, none too subtly, displaced Russo's leadership of the group with himself. He was the dean, after all. And he would be the one taking over as president when Stegall suffered his inevitable disability.

"Fine, how're y'all?" said Perry Moon. He ducked his head. R. D. shoved a drink in his hand. Moon stood looking around for a chair.

"Sit here," R. D. said, indicating a straight chair against the wall.

"Yes sir," Moon said, and sat. He seemed sullen and distracted.

Who is this boy?, Jefferson thought. He knew him only by name. His face was vaguely familiar from the new faculty reception at Flower Hill the previous September. But he couldn't remember seeing him on campus at all after that. Maybe Moon was always *off* campus doing whatever the hell it was that social work people did.

"We were just discussing perhaps inviting a woman faculty member to join our group," the dean said.

"Oh?" said Moon.

"Maybe you have a suggestion," Jefferson said.

"Well..." he said. He looked around at all the other men. He looked as though he felt trapped, as if they were somehow testing him.

"Relax, Perry," the dean said, warmly using the young man's given name. "We're all the same here. Assistant professors are equal to full professors."

"Huh," said Dobbs.

"We are just men on a mission," Jefferson said, ignoring Dobbs. "We are racking our brains, trying to come up with the appropriate woman."

"Who needs a split-tail?" Dobbs asked.

"Fred, you've made your feelings amply clear," the dean said. "Please refrain from misogynistic remarks."

"Shit!" said Dobbs.

"We need a woman, or two or three, Fred, because this faculty is made up of almost fifty percent female. We need the woman's point of view for balance. I must say—even though I don't like your choice of words—that I agree with you to an extent; but there are strong women on this faculty, and some must be of like mind with us."

"How about Willow Behn?" said Katz.

"Shit, that bull-dyke is a screaming liberal!" Dobbs said.

"Liberal or not, I don't care," said Katz, "she might hate Stegall as much as we do. Who cares if she's, as you say, 'liberal'? It makes no difference; it just might be in our favor."

"She's not cozy with him, I know that," R. D. put in.

"How do you know that, R.D.?" Dobbs asked.

"From some of the things I've heard her say. She's a free spirit.

She doesn't like taking orders from anybody, especially a man like Stegall."

"No, she doesn't," the dean interjected. "Are there any other suggestions?"

"What about Lucille Willard?" R. D. said. "She's getting rich writing that history of Florida; every high school in the state uses it."

"What's that got to do with anything?" Perry Moon said, in his high, screeching voice, and they all looked at him as if he had suddenly farted.

After a moment, R. D. said, "Nothing. I was just making conversation."

"Let's stay on task, gentlemen," the dean said. Russo glared at him. *The man does hates me*, the dean thought, *and he is dangerous. I must be careful.* "Willow Behn and Lucy Willard," he said, "they both live in Bostony House I believe. Anybody else?"

"How about Lily Putnam? Seriously," R. D. said.

"Put it back in your britches, R. D.," Dobbs said, and all the men laughed.

"She *is* a bright young woman," the dean said, "but I don't know."

"She's the best looking woman to be on this faculty in a long, long time," Fred Dobbs said.

"How is that important to anything?" Garcia Russo scoffed. He looked with disdain at Jefferson. "Let's listen to our *leader*," he said, mockingly. "Dean Jefferson, you have the floor." He sneered.

"I've had the floor for some time, Garcia," Jefferson said, "if you haven't noticed."

"I've been here the whole time! I've *noticed*!" Russo said.

"Well, my friend, would you like the floor now? Better yet, why don't you preside over the meeting?"

"You're doing just fine for a fucking dean," Garcia said. "What about your better half? Dr. Paulette Jefferson?"

"Well, she's certainly of like mind with me," Jefferson said. "We're two peas in a pod." *Paulette would crack me over the head if she ever heard me say that!* the dean thought. "She'll be with us, of course. That goes without saying."

"Then why say it?" Garcia jeered.

"Just a figure of speech, Dr. Russo," Jefferson said.

"Then I declare this meeting adjourned," Garcia said. "R. D., fill the glasses and turn on the teevee!"

"Wait a minute," R. D. said. "Okay, in a second. But we never decided on a woman!"

"We will, R. D., we will," Russo said, holding up his glass. "Next meeting. And next time, *Dean* Jefferson, bring Maker's Mark again, and not this cheap stuff. "

Jefferson said nothing. *These bastards are going to bleed me for every last drop, but I need them. I need them.*

It was a rainy, stormy afternoon, and Lily and Brass were sitting at a table inside Stache's, having a drink after their last classes of the day. The thunderstorm was one of those windy squalls that came in off the Gulf from time to time to disturb the usual calm and tranquil Panhandle weather. The inside of Stache's was crowded, since the blowing rain kept people off the porch.

"What is that?" Finch asked Randy when he took their orders, pointing to a machine that had been newly installed in the corner. There seemed to be some kind of screen and a microphone.

"Karaoke machine," Randy said.

"Oh, my god," Finch said, "this will never do. You must tell Cheryl to take it out!" Cheryl was the owner and manager of Stache's; her husband was chairman of the philosophy department.

"Yes sir, I'll tell her," Randy said, "but some of the students wanted it."

"What'll happen to this?" Finch asked, pointing to a speaker overhead, from which came the smooth sounds of the Dave Brubeck quartet.

"Nothing, it'll still be here," Randy said, leaving to get their drinks.

"Shit," Finch said to Lily.

"Maybe it won't be too bad, Brass," she said. "It might be fun."

"That's not my idea of fun," he said.

When they had their drinks and had taken a few sips, Finch said, "You were really awesome in the play, Lily. You were simply dazzling."

"How can one be 'simply' dazzling?" she asked with a smile. "But thank you, Brass. You're sweet to keep telling me I was good."

"No, really," he said, "I think you should consider a career on the stage."

"You're kidding."

"No, I'm not. You were that good."

"Well...thanks, but..."

"You're wasting yourself grading all those papers, sitting on interminable committees. You deserve better," Finch said. He pressed her hand on the table.

"You're sweet, Brass. And I love you. But..."

Just then two girls got up and went over to the Karaoke machine. They twirled some dials and the Brubeck jazz went mute.

"Oh, fuck," Brass said. "Here it comes. Goddammit!"

"Shhhh," Lily shushed her drinking companion. "They'll hear you."

"I don't give a flying fuck," Brass said.

The two girls looked like sorority sisters. They both wore knee length skirts, one brown, the other blue, similar light cream colored sweaters. They were about the same height, one blonde, the other more strawberry blonde, and they wore their hair shoulder length and shiny.

"The Bobbsey Twins," Brass said under his breath. Lily was pleased that he whispered it.

Suddenly the banging opening piano chords of what was unmistakably "Bad, Bad Leroy Brown" came booming out of the speakers. Finch wondered if they were going to sing along with Jim Croce, then realized that it was only the music, for them to sing with.

The girls began tapping their feet and clapping their hands. They launched into "On the south side of Chicago/ in the baddest part of town..." Their voices were shrill and tinny. When they got to the chorus they sang, "The baddest man in the whole *darn* town/badder than old King Kong, meaner than a junkyard dog."

"Oh my god," Brass said and pressed his hand against his forehead. Lily tugged at his arm. "Deliver me," he said.

"Brass..." she whispered, "no. Calm down."

"They're ruining the song!" he said, "they're cutting the balls off of it. 'Whole *'darn'* town, Jesus Christ!" They sat listening to the girls sing, watching them trying to get other customers to clap along with them. Some did. They seemed immensely pleased with themselves.

They finished to scattered applause. When they finally ended what Brass thought was a complete bowdlerization of poor Jim Croce's song, the jazz came back on over the speakers. The two girls were crossing the room, accepting compliments from other students.

"They don't know what a junkyard dog is," Brass said, "or even a junkyard. They've probably never even seen one."

"Shhhh," she said, patting his hand as the girls came closer.

"Ladies!" Finch said, and they stopped and looked at him.

"Yes sir?" they said in unison.

"You two girls were in fine voice this evening," he said.

"Thank you sir," one of them said. The other looked suspicious, hearing Brass's tone of voice. Lily let out her breath; *maybe he will behave.*

"On the south side of Chicago—have you ever been there, girls?—I thought not; in that culture, in that milieu that Mr. Croce, God rest his soul, was writing about, one would never, ever say 'darn' town. You changed his lyrics. It should be, now and forever, whole *damn* town!"

"Yes sir," the girl said. The other remained silent. "Is he dead?"

"Yes mam, deader than old King Kong, and I suspect he is turning over in his grave just about now. Jim Croce was killed in a plane crash several years ago. But his memory lives on, in the music and the lyrics of his songs, and it is not for us to tamper with them. Do you understand?"

"Yes sir," the girl said.

*Stop **now**, Brass*, Lily thought.

"To say 'darn' rather than 'damn' takes the *soul* out of his song," Finch went on. "It is totally out of keeping with the world he was writing about. 'Darn' is so vanilla, so Methodist!"

"We *are* Methodists," the girl who had been quiet up to then said.

"Well, good for you," Finch said. "I hope the next time you sing that song—which is decidedly *not* Methodist—you'll take what I'm saying into consideration."

"Yes sir," in unison, and moving away. Backing away, quickly.

When they were gone, Lily said,

"Brass, was that necessary?"

"It was a teaching moment, Lily, and a learning moment for them."

They were silent for a few moments, sipping their drinks. "You know, Brass," she said, "you can really be an arrogant son-of-a-bitch."

He laughed. He drained his glass and chuckled. Holding his glass up he shouted to Randy, making a circle in the air with his other hand, "Another round, good fellow!"

When they had their second drinks, Finch said,

"Do *you* know what a junkyard dog is? Have you ever seen a junkyard?"

"Well, there was a big vacant lot in Gilbertown with a lot of old equipment rusting in it. I guess that was junk."

"Did it have a fence around it?"

"No, I don't think so."

"Then it wasn't a junkyard. A junkyard dog roamed the inside of the fence of a real junkyard and would snarl and snap at anybody who came near. Meaner than hell. Anybody who broke in he would tear limb from limb! You didn't mess with a junkyard dog."

"I'll file that away, Brasfield, in my treasure trove of trivia."

"Very clever," he said, chortling again. He was really in a good mood. "My treasure trove of trivia! Beautiful! I'll file *that* one away."

"You seem to feel very good today."

"Yes, unlike most people, rainy days get me *up*!" He smiled. He looked around the crowded bar. "These students," he said, "they're innocent. They don't know any better."

"Any better than what?"

"Any better than to be innocent." He sipped his drink. "That girl there, smoking the cigarette. She thinks she's hot shit, but she really *would* be hot shit if she didn't so obviously think so."

"I see what you mean," she said.

"She's so innocent she's phony. She doesn't know any better." He looked at Lily, his brown eyes twinkling. "But enough about students, the loathsome creatures we spend our limited time on earth and our life's energies with; I suppose you're looking forward to Charlie Stewart and the Yancey Lectures."

"Oh, yes," she said. They had received the overall title of his series of four lectures: "How Can We Know the Dancer From the Dance?" She was fascinated; she loved Yeats's poem "Among School Children." It had become one of her favorites in her reading to prepare herself for the visiting scholar. "The body is not bruised to pleasure soul/ Nor beauty born out of its own despair/ Nor bleareyed wisdom out of midnight oil." She could read Yeats over and over and never tire of him.

"I suppose you're getting horny," he said.

"Brass!" she said. "I'm looking forward to his discussion of the poems. The man may not even like me. He might be gay or something, or happily married."

"'Happily married,' dear, is an oxymoron. And I can assure you he is not gay. He never even once made a pass at me, and I found him scrumptious, almost made me wish I *was* gay."

"He's a lot younger than you, isn't he?"

"Of course, but not as much younger than you are than me, and *you* made a pass at me."

"*I* made a pass at *you*? Revisionist history, my man." They laughed together.

"Anyway, what does it matter? The focus now should be on Dr. Charles Stewart, and how you're going to get into his britches."

"I don't think I'll have much trouble, unless he's...well...you know."

"I don't expect you will, darling. He is human, and he is male. He puts on his jockstrap like everybody else."

"His 'jockstrap?' I thought the saying was 'puts on his socks.'"

"I think jockstrap is more appropriate in this case. Don't you?" Finch asked.

She paused. She shook her head and grinned. "I suppose so, Brass, I suppose so. But I'm looking forward to his lectures."

"I've never been much on poetry, to tell you the truth," Finch said. " Yeats, yes. But this contemporary stuff is gibberish to me; I can't understand it. It's as though the poet's first duty is to obfuscate, not communicate. And poetry has far too few words for my taste. Give me a good chunk of prose fiction anytime. Poetry is like nibbling Melba toast when I want about a one-fourth portion of a fat pecan pie!"

Lily laughed heartedly. "You are something else, Brass," she said, "you are something else."

CHAPTER ELEVEN

Dean Wallace Jefferson spent most of his days ruminating about President John Stegall's oncoming crisis, which was on schedule even though the dull Stegall had not a clue as to the catastrophe's imminence.

Across the quad, in his palatial office, John Stegall sat wondering how that fat asshole Jefferson had found out about his dementia; it was getting worse, and his doctor had increased the dosage of both Namenda and Aricept, but he was determined not to let it get him down. He had told no one about it, not even Nelle; she probably wouldn't hear him anyway, so busy was she with her day lilies. But he suspected the dean had somehow found out; maybe it was that damned doctor, and he would be looking at a lawsuit if it was him, by damn!

Dean Jefferson sat doodling on a yellow legal pad on his desk. He was somewhat frustrated by the group of rebels he had organized, though "organized" was perhaps too strong a word for it.

Garcia Russo's suggestion: "Maybe we should get some students to streak again. Run naked through his office."

"Not a bad idea," Jefferson had said contemplatively. *But who was going to put a student up to it? I can't do such a thing; if it got out it would be terrible for me*, the dean thought. "Do you know any students who might be gently prodded to do so?" he had asked Russo.

"No," Russo said. No further comment.

"Maybe we could turn loose a bunch of snakes in the fucker's office," Fred C. Dobbs said. "That ought to get him going good!"

"Or fire ants," Bob Lallo said. He had joined them at their last meeting. They had decided to ask Lillian Lallo, who was immediate past chairperson of the faculty senate, to come to a meeting, but she had declined. Bob had accepted, though most of the other men would not have invited him because he was such a milquetoast.

"Fire ants!?" said Dobbs. "Get serious, Bob!"

"What's wrong with fire ants?" Bob asked defensively.

"Are *you* going to pick up a bunch of fire ants and carry them over there?! Good luck!" Dobbs exclaimed.

"Well, are *you* going to carry a bunch of snakes over there?"

"Hell, yeah! I got a cage full of cottonmouths in my lab in Harmon. Piece of cake!" Dobbs said smugly. "I'll do it tomorrow if you want me to," he said, directing his remark to the whole group.

"Let's do it," Katz said.

"Cottonmouths are poisonous," the dean said, "several bites could be fatal."

"Naw. These are de-fanged and milked, Dean-o. All bark, no bite."

"They'll just *scare* the hell out of him," R. D. Wettermark said. "We don't want to *kill* the little shrimp."

"We could kidnap Olive Hoyle, his squeeze," Perry Moon said, "take her off and tie her up and blind-fold her."

"You've been watching too many movies, Perry," Katz said. "Why would we want to do that? You want to get the cops involved?"

"No, no," Moon said, "it was just a suggestion."

"Another rape on campus ought to do the trick," Alexander Daniels said.

"Who did you have in mind, Alex," Wettermark said, "Miss Putnam?"

"Not an altogether bad idea," Jefferson said. "A rape, I mean. Not Miss Putnam, for heaven's sakes. Maybe we could get Brasfield Finch on a statutory rape charge."

"You mean that drunk bastard is banging *that*?!" R. D. said.

"No, no, no. Lily Putnam is twenty six years old. I mean a student, under age. Just to create a scandal," the dean said. *He probably is banging her*, Jefferson thought uneasily. It was the first time the thought had occurred to him, and it made him irritably furious and resentful, as if he suddenly knew for a fact that Finch was dabbling where he himself so longed to dabble. "He drinks so much," Jefferson went on, "that he probably can't even get it up." *Would that that was so*, he thought.

"Then how can he rape somebody?" Perry Moon said.

"Never mind, Perry," the dean said impatiently, "let's get off that. I don't think that's quite the right path, anyway."

"Let's do the snakes!" Katz said.

"Okay, okay," Jefferson said, "we'll think about it. Everybody try to come up with other ideas, okay? In the meantime, Fred, keep your snakes ready!"

They settled on the snakes, and in the dead of night Fred C. Dobbs and R. D. Wettermark crept over to Woodfin Hall with a large crate. The building was locked, of course, but R. D. had a master key he had gotten from Ernest Jones, one of the men in charge of maintenance; Jones and R. D. were drinking buddies. The master key would open any building and office on campus. "Maybe we ought to check out some other offices while we're at it," R. D. said. "Shit, R. D.," said Dobbs, "let's just get this one done." They put the snakes around in Stegall's shadowy office as if they were hiding Easter eggs. They giggled while they were doing it. Desk drawers, filing cabinets. R. D. wanted to look through some of the president's files, but Dobbs wouldn't let him. "We got to get out of here before old Puckett makes his rounds," he said. Ernest Puckett was the campus security officer, a retired Church of Christ minister. Ernest wanted to carry a gun but the administration wouldn't let him. He wore a uniform, but for a weapon he had to be satisfied with a sawed-off pool cue which he carried like a billyclub. "Hurry, hurry," Dobbs kept saying. "Won't Ernest find the snakes?" R. D. asked. "Shit, R. D., he just checks the outside doors and goes back to the gate house and goes to sleep."

"How do you know that?"

"Because I *know* it, goddammit!"

President Stegall woke up in his upstairs bedroom at Flower Hill. He could smell coffee perking; his black cook and maid, Betsy Roundtree, who was actually an employee of the caf but was assigned to the president's home, was already in the kitchen downstairs. Stegall stretched in his big king sized bed and farted. Twice. That was one reason, other than his snoring, that Nelle, his wife, slept in a separate bedroom. "You keep me awake all night and then stink me out in the morning," she had said, "no thanks." *Good riddance*, Stegall had thought. *If a woman can't stand a little morning gas, then she* should *sleep elsewhere.* He was happy to have the big bed to himself.

John sat up on the edge of his bed; he wore crisp blue pajamas that Betsy Roundtree washed and ironed for him every day. That was one of the perks of his office, by damn, and he took advantage of every perk he could. *I am President*, he thought. *I am the president, and no one should ever forget it.* He looked at his medicine in its plastic box on the bedside table; he had to take a handful of pills every morning, and he didn't even know what half of them were. His blood pressure medicine. Other heart medicine. (His doctors had told him last summer that he had developed Congestive Heart Failure, which alarmed him at first until they assured him it could be controlled with medication. He had to be careful: no salt, and his usual sausage patty was verboten, though he said to hell with it and had one every morning anyway, along with his poached egg on an English muffin. He didn't tell Nelle or anyone else about that diagnosis of CHF either; he kept it as secret as he did his dementia. It was nobody's business but his. And that damned nosy dean, who seemed to have made it *his* business.)

In the kitchen, dressed in one of his blue, pin-striped suits—which Betsy Roundtree had cleaned and pressed every day so that he always had a selection of suits that were tidy and spruced to choose from—with a purple and gold striped tie and an American flag in the lapel of the jacket, Stegall sat alone in the sunny breakfast nook. He had his usual half a cup of black coffee and his poached egg. He did not make small talk with Betsy Roundtree. His wife was still asleep upstairs; she sometimes slept until ten or eleven, before she arose and went about her hobby with the day lilies. It was quiet and peaceful in the kitchen, and Stegall sat contemplating his life. He had risen much higher than his drunken father had ever thought he would, and he was annoyed that the mean old man hadn't lived to see him become The President. His mother was in a nursing home with severe dementia; she didn't even know who John was when he went to visit her. She couldn't appreciate the heights to which he had risen, either. And Nelle was so busy with her day lilies that she didn't seem at all impressed with him. Stegall could not imagine her not getting bored with her hobby; he, himself, could not have lasted two minutes with day lilies, or any other kinds of flowers, for that matter. Nelle was a woman on a mission. He would have thought she would have long since covered every vacant spot of ground on the campus and in the town of Lakewood, but she was still going at it. It was to be her legacy. Stegall chortled to himself; *some legacy!* The woman was a fussbudget; he was glad she had something to keep her out of his hair.

He strolled across the campus in the cool of the winter morning, greeting early rising students as he passed them, checking on the maintenance men as they worked in the azalea beds. He breathed deeply the fresh Florida air, smelling the Gulf on the breeze. It was a fine day. High, wispy clouds against the early sun. This academic year had been so much calmer and saner than last year, and for that he was grateful. Not one single meddling reporter from a Tallahassee

TV station, on campus trying to get a story. The publicity from last year's events had been devastating to him; he had asked his cardiologist if perhaps that trauma had brought on his Congestive Heart Failure. The fool child-man of a doctor had laughed and told him that no, he'd probably had the condition for some time, years, maybe. But Stegall knew better than that wet-behind-the-ears physician; he knew where it had come from.

Eloise Hoyle was already at her desk and greeted him amicably. "It's a fantastic day, Eloise," he said, passing into his own office. She agreed loudly. He sat behind his enormous, heavy desk and pumped up his chair. He never knew when that boob of a fathead Dean Jefferson might come sniffing around, and he wanted to be ready.

There was a pad of his lavender notes in the middle of his blotter ("Office of the President, John W. Stegall, PhD," in raised gold letters) and he opened the middle drawer and took out his favorite Cross pen and began to doodle on the top page. He drew a box with a triangle inside. He went on to other shapes, whistling under his breath.

Idly, he opened the second drawer in his desk and looked in. There was a stack of his lavender note pads in there, and he took them out and counted them. Only five left. He would have to get Eloise to call the printers and order some more. His eyes wandered to the back of the drawer, and there, curled up and staring at him with cold and malevolent eyes, was a large snake; he closed the drawer carefully. He had dreamed last night of snakes curling around day lilies, and he assumed this was a flashback to his dream; there could not possibly be a snake in his office drawer.

Just then he heard a ruckus on the stairs in the foyer that led up to the second floor. It sounded like the large, cumbersome shoes of Billy "Big Hoss" Murphy, the dean of men. *I really should have had an elevator put in*, thought Stegall. The turbulence sounded as though Murphy was falling down the stairs. *What in the world?*

"Goddammit, there's a fucking *snake* in my office!" he heard the man bellow.

"A *snake*?" he heard Eloise Hoyle shriek. Then, in a calmer tone, "Surely you're mistaken, Dean Murphy," she said.

"No, I'm not! He was right there, on the carpet. Looking at me!"

"Sometimes that happens in Florida," Eloise said.

"Fuck! Not to *me* it doesn't! Call maintenance. Call security." Stegall imagined old Ernest Puckett beating the snake over the head with his stick. *A snake!?* Stegall cautiously reopened his drawer. There it was, slick and black, still in the same position looking at him as if it knew who he was. *Jesus, Mary and Joseph*! thought the president, closing the drawer again.

"Eloise!" he howled. "Get in here!"

"What?!" she said, sticking her head in the door.

"There's a s…sn…snake in my desk drawer! Get him out!"

"I'm afraid of snakes," she said. She stood there wringing her hands.

"Big Hoss" barged into the room. "You, too, John?!" he said, "what the fuck?"

"There is no cause for vulgarity, Mr. Murphy," Stegall said. He sat high in his chair, holding his feet off the floor. He held the second drawer of his desk firmly shut.

"Look! There's another one!" Murphy said. A long, fat snake was slithering across the carpet. Murphy climbed onto a visitor's chair and pulled his feet up. "What the fuck, John?!" he exclaimed, "it's Alfred Hitchcock!"

"What?! Don't be silly, Hoss," Stegall said. To Eloise, who was shrinking in the doorway, her eyes wide, he said, "Go. Call maintenance and security."

"Yes, sir," she said and disappeared. They heard her scream, "Oh My God! There's one in here. I'm getting out of here!"

They heard the outside door slam to behind her.

"Pick up the phone, John!" Murphy said. "Call them yourself! Shit!" Another snake wriggled across the floor. "Where the hell they all coming from?!"

John dialed the extension for security, and Ernest Puckett answered. "This is John Stegall," the president said, his voice shaking, "snakes are running rampant in Woodfin Hall! Get over here, right away."

"Snakes?" asked Puckett. He sounded suspicious, as though he thought someone was pulling his leg.

"Yes, Snakes! They are everywhere. Call maintenance and get some men over here, right now!"

"Yes, sir," Puckett said. He hung up.

"Goddammit it all, John," Murphy said. "Call Alberta and tell her not to come in." Alberta Wingate was the dean of women.

John did so. She seemed relieved—and not at all surprised—when he told her and hung up quickly. "You think Alberta had anything to do with this?" he asked Murphy.

"Who? Alberta? Not a chance. Somebody, but not Alberta."

The two men watched several snakes gliding across the floor. *Those awful people in Harmon*, thought Stegall. And he was sure that that gross, meaty butterball Wallace Jefferson had something to do with it, too. Two of the snakes seemed to be playing with one another. They became all twined together.

"You think they're fucking?" Murphy asked.

"I'm sure I don't know," Stegall said huffily.

"Just wondering," said Murphy. "They look like moccasins to me. Probably water or cottonmouth. I knew a man got bitten by a water moccasin and he was dead before he could get back to his boat. They found him floating face down. They're some mean motherfuckers."

"Yes, I suppose they are," Stegall said. Stegall's legs were getting cramped from holding them above the floor. He could feel his pulse beating in his ears. *My blood pressure must be sky high*, he thought. "Where *are* they?" he asked. "It's taking them a long time to get here." His hands were trembling. *Damn them, I'll fire them all!*

They heard a stirring in the outer office. Ernest Puckett came through the door dressed in a white hazmat suit with a canvas helmet and a net over his face. He had his stick and a wire basket. "Where are they?" he asked.

"Damn, Earl, where'd you get all that shit?" Murphy asked.

"It was left over from when me and the pest control people got the bats out of the attic of Ferguson Hall," he said. "Comes in handy, huh? Where are they?"

"Just look down, Mr. Puckett, and you'll see them. Be careful," Stegall said. "Don't get yourself bitten." It occurred to him then that the college might be liable for any harm that came to anybody. "Are you sure that suit's enough to protect you?"

"It's like steel, Dr. Stegall," Puckett said. He swatted at a snake on the floor and hit it across the head; the snake looked stunned and rolled over. The old man smoothly glided the inert snake into the wire cage. "I'll get them, Dr. Stegall, don't you worry," he said. "I'll kill ever one of them."

Two men arrived from maintenance. One of them had a long stick with a looped wire on the end. "This here's a snake catcher," he said. He expertly wrapped the wire around the necks of the two snakes who were entwined; he lifted them together into Puckett's basket.

"Are they fucking?" Murphy asked the men.

"I don't know, Mr. Murphy," one of them said.

"There's one in my desk drawer," Stegall said. His voice sounded hollow and tinny in his ears.

"We'll get it, Dr. Stegall," the talkative one said. "Why don't you and Mr. Murphy go on outside for a while? We'll get them all."

As the president walked out of the building, his legs were stiff, tingling and unsteady. He held onto "Hoss" Murphy's elbow as they descended the steps outside. A crowd had gathered. "Go back to your classrooms and offices," he said, "the crisis is over. We have survived." He was short of breath, and he breathed in as deeply as he could. He felt light-headed. He was not at all sure *he* had survived.

CHAPTER TWELVE

Brasfield Finch heard some students out in the hall talking about the snakes in Woodfin Hall. His immediate thought was that someone had put them there, and the only person on campus he could think of who might have done it was Fred C. Dobbs, the local expert on serpents. Fred often bragged about his snakes; on several occasions he had appeared on campus with one of them twined around his arm, causing pandemonium among the other faculty, especially the ladies. Fred would laugh uproariously as though he thought it was the funniest thing he'd ever seen. If someone had indeed planted them, Fred would be the likeliest suspect. Finch thought he was probably too moronic to realize that.

Finch had just had his first snort of Chivas Regal for the day. He settled back, breathing the fresh breeze that came through his windows. He had chosen, that morning, a bright pink cord to tie around the bottom of his fulsome, effusive beard, of which he was most proud. Its bushiness covered his chest and came down to his waist, where it narrowed to a point that was always tied with a colorful piece of string.

Finch sensed the presence of someone in the doorway; he looked up and there stood a boy who was vaguely familiar to him. He could not place his face. The boy—perhaps man, he seemed to be a little older than the average student—smiled at Finch. "Good morning, Mr. Finch," he said. He wore khaki pants and a blue and red madras shirt. His head was almost shaved; he had an extreme buzz cut, his hair so short it looked like fuzz on his head. "How are you?"

"Fine and dandy," Finch said, "how are you?"

"Not fine," the boy said, with the crooked smile, "and not dandy." He just stood there, looking down at Finch. A full minute passed and the boy said nothing.

"Is there something I can help you with?" Finch asked.

"Well, no. Probably. I mean, maybe, yeah."

Another minute went by. The boy made Finch uneasy. "Do I know you, Mr...uh...?"

"Yeah, you know me."

Then it hit Finch in the face like a ton of confetti. Rudolph Cowan! His face was fleshier, but his eyes, the smile, the same. Cowan's smile broadened. "Yeah," he said, and nodded his head, "it's me." Rudolph had had hair down to his shoulders when he'd been in Finch's writing class. He was much younger then. *How many years had it been?* Finch was not sure. *What had the tv people said?*

"Well," Finch said, suddenly wishing he had had another snort, "long time, no see. How long has it been?"

"A good while," Cowan said. "I bet it seemed longer to me than it did to you."

"Mr. Cowan, you...well, I suppose you have served your time, or whatever," Brasfield said.

"Whatever. It wasn't no fun," Cowan said. "They fuck with your mind in there. They give you a jolt of electricity, fucks you up. You don't know up from down for a while. But I got better. I got *cured.*"

"Yes, well...that's good," Finch said uncomfortably. A full minute of silence. "I suppose you're ready to start your life anew," he said, with false heartiness. The expression on Cowan's face did not change. He seemed to enjoy the long, pregnant pauses.

"Whatever," he finally said.

"Are you...coming back to school?"

"Maybe. Maybe not."

"Well, I don't have any room in my workshop next semester," Finch said. "I'm sorry."

"I figured that would be the case," Cowan said. He seemed to have a habit of sticking the tip of his tongue out and running it around his lips. "Probably no room in the inn at all."

"Sorry?"

"Never mind, Mr. Finch. Relax. I ain't going to try to get into your writing class. I've already had it, remember? I forget what grade I made. Ancient history. Hey, you still hitting the bottle? Yeah. I smell it. When I got locked away I didn't forget what it smells like. When you get out it seems like your sense of smell is stronger, you know? So I smell you." He sniffed the air. "I'd put a buck on it that it's Scotch."

"Yes," Finch said. He started to ask him if he wanted a hit, then thought the better of it. The sooner he could get rid of this nut the better. "Well, I really must..."

"I know," Cowan said, "you must pretend to read manuscripts. What do you do in here all day besides drink? Beat your meat?"

"Mr. Cowan, I hardly think that's appropriate," Finch said. Cowan did not respond. "Really," Finch said, "I must get to work, even though you are sure I do nothing all day. Is that all you wanted?"

"Yeah," he said. "Don't work too hard." He slouched there for a few moments. "I'll see you," he said, "I'll be around."

Yes, I'll bet you will, thought Finch. "Good day, Mr. Cowan," he said.

"Yeah," Cowan said, and disappeared from the doorway. Finch got out his bottle and poured himself a hefty drink. He looked at the empty doorway, expecting Cowan to suddenly re-appear, but he didn't.

Finch tapped lightly on the inside frame of Lily's office door; the girl was hunched over her desk marking papers, her red pen gripped tightly in her fingers. She looked up. Her bare legs were spread under the desk, her tiny green skirt barely covering her goodies. She sat like a sailor on a bench; *just crawl around under there and take a good peek*, Finch thought. Then he realized that he not only couldn't, but didn't have to, crawl anywhere to see her prize; he could see it anytime he wanted. He smiled. "Good day, sweet lady," he said.

"Oh, Brass," she said, turning. "Tell me you're going to get me away from these infernal papers!"

"Yes, my fair one, we are going over to welcome Charlie Stewart to the campus. Come on."

"He's *here?*" she said.

"Yes, got in this morning. He is well ensconced in the apartment in Hill House. Let's walk over there." Hill House was on the edge of campus and was the former home of the Home Economics Department, equipped with a large kitchen, dining room, and den for relaxing. The attached apartment was a nicely appointed one bedroom, once the bailiwick of Miss Sara Nell Darksey, the longtime chairperson of that now depleted and exhausted department that taught young ladies how to be proper housewives. The demand for the courses had waned, Miss Darksey had retired, and Hill House had been turned into an entertainment facility, with some offices; Miss Darksey's old apartment was given over to visiting scholars and artists who would be on campus for several days, sometimes longer. Dr. Charles Stewart would be there for a week, giving four public lectures and meeting with students.

"I instructed Eloise Hoyle to lay in a good supply of Scotch," Finch said, as they walked, "Stewart's preferred drink." Finch carried his old scuffed, worn leather briefcase that he rarely used. "No telling what she bought, so I'm bringing him a bottle of Glenlivet to brighten his day. Nothing like a touch of single malt to welcome a traveler! And we'll get to drink it, too. Joyful day, huh?"

Lily was nervous about meeting the man. She had let the anticipation get out of hand. *He puts on his jockstrap like anyone else;* remembering Brass's remark did not help matters. She had looked carefully and closely at Stewart's picture; *but what if he's hair-lipped or something worse?* She was in awe of the man's scholarship, his writing about W. B. Yeats. She had never known a really famous scholar before; she was aware that Willow had made a splash with her book on Byron years ago, but she was not "famous" famous. She was Lily's friend, more or less just a colleague.

"He's a Mormon," Lily blurted to Finch.

"I beg your pardon?" Finch said.

"A Mormon. A fucking Mormon."

"No, no, Lily," Finch said. "Not a *practicing* Mormon. They don't allow Mormons to teach at Harvard."

"Well, they allow this one."

"Relax, dear. Charlie is not really into the Church of The Latter Day Saints, trust me on that. Mormons are not permitted to drink alcohol; Charlie would flunk that Canon in a New York minute! And he's a well-known womanizer. He has no need for multiple wives."

"You didn't tell me that," Lily said.

"That he's a womanizer? Why else am I setting you up for him, or him for *you*, if you prefer. It'll be a fun idyll, and then you'll both go your merry ways!"

"I'm not real comfortable with this, Brass," she said. They were almost to Hill House.

"I can't imagine why not," he said. "He's just a man with a dick, Lily. All that Yeats shit is just froufrou."

"I have a hard time wrapping my brain around that one, Brass," she said.

Brass was knocking on the outside door of the apartment. The door swung open and there stood Dr. Charles Stewart, eminent Yeats scholar, Yancey Lecturer. Lily was a bit taken aback; he was a good looking man, but he didn't look the way he did in the photograph. His dark hair was different, combed over his forehead; and he was only an inch or two taller than she was, probably five foot eight or so. She had somehow had the impression that he was taller, though his photo had been a head and shoulders shot against a crammed book-case. She did not *mind* that he was shorter, she was just a bit startled to see him face to face. He had the collar of his white, oxford cloth button down open at the neck, and he held a glass in his hand.

"Welcome to my lair," he said, smiling, and he and Finch did a male hug, a chest bump and pats on the shoulders. "How have you been, my friend?"

"As well as could be expected for an old fart," Finch said, moving into the living room. He held Lily by the elbow.

"And who is this delectable creature?" Stewart said, eying Lily.

"This is my friend and colleague Lily Putnam," Finch said, "she has come to welcome you to Lakewood."

"Well, I feel welcomed already," Stewart said. "Come in and have a drink. The whiskey's decent, Johnny Walker Black."

Finch had been afraid Eloise would buy Usher's House or something on that level. "Ah, old friend," Finch said, "I bring you single malt!" and he pulled the bottle out of his satchel.

"You are a scholar and a gentleman, Brasfield Finch," Stewart said.

"Neither, I'm afraid," Finch said, "but let's have a drink of this lovely nectar. Lily?"

"Of course," she said, and Stewart smiled at her. *Love has pitched its tent…* she thought.

They settled with their drinks, she and Finch on the couch. Stewart eyeballed her legs, perusing them with obvious pleasure. His glance dawdled on her breasts. "My, my, where did you find *her*, Finch?" he asked.

"She is my colleague," Finch said, "assistant professor of English."

"Oh. Really? They don't make assistant professors as concupiscent as this where I come from." He chortled. *Concupiscent?* "She is rare," he said to Finch, as though Lily weren't sitting right there, then he turned to her. "Your degree? Where from?"

"I don't have my doctorate," Lily said. "I'm ABD. Emory."

"Excellent school," he said. "Your dissertation is on…?"

"Toni Morrison," she said.

"Excellent. Excellent." She uncrossed her legs, then re-crossed them. He watched intently. "Excellent," he said again; she assumed he meant her legs. He was focused on where her tight mini-skirt crossed her thighs, probably imagining her "mouse's ear," as her mother had called it when she was a little girl. She had no idea why that long ago euphemism had popped into her head.

"Thank you," she said, not knowing what else to say. She took a sip of the smooth, *excellent* whiskey. Stewart and Finch began to reminisce—like fraternity boys—about their drunken evening in New York at the Algonquin. It gave her a chance to more closely check the man out. He was thin and wiry, and—yes indeed!—that hair was a comb-over. His bio had said he was thirty nine years old, but he looked a few years older. His face was like that of a man who had recently lost a lot of weight, gaunt, his features sharp and severe. But he was extremely handsome, sexy; his body, though slender, looked solid and hard. *He will not be at all bad*, thought Lily.

Stewart and Finch were well into their second or third drinks. Lily looked at her watch. "Oh," she said, "the time! Dr. Stewart, you have a meeting with students at four."

"I can't meet with students when I've been drinking," he said cheerfully, "and call me Charlie."

"That never stopped Brass," she said, "Charlie."

"Actually, dear, I just don't feel like it. I'm tired from the flight, and that ride from the airport to the campus in that beat-up college station wagon almost did me in. I think that student driver was high as a kite."

"Very likely," Finch said. "Lily, go over to Comer Auditorium and dismiss them. Tell them Dr. Stewart is not feeling well."

"They'll be disappointed," Lily said.

"I doubt it," Finch said.

"Their professors have prepared them for this," Lily said, "I know *I* have. Everybody's been reading Yeats."

"Very good," Stewart said. "In good time, darling. We'll get around to the old boy. Billy Butler can wait. He's not going any-where. In the meantime, tell me more about yourself, dear girl."

"Well, I have to go over and tell them you're not coming,"

Lily said.

"Oh, let them sit. They'll figure it out. They'll probably *stampede* out of there."

Lily was annoyed at his attitude. "I don't think so," she said, "not my students, anyway. They *love* the Yeats I've read them. I gave them copies of some of the poems. They're eager. I even Xeroxed one of your papers from the *Yale Review* and they read it and discussed it. They're ready for you," she said. "Charlie," she added.

"Oh dear," Stewart said, "I'm afraid I've upset the beautiful assistant professor."

"Don't worry about it," Finch said.

Lily was furious with both of them. They talked about her as if she were a piece of handsome furniture in the room. She was thinking as she walked over to Comer: *I am defined by neither 'beautiful' nor 'assistant professor.' I am more than that. I'm not an object with a label. I am a woman with a brain! And feelings. She knew they didn't mean to treat her that way, and that's what made her so sad. That was the problem with men; they had not a clue who or what they were.* She felt pity for Charlie Stewart. For both of them. *They were all the same. Men. They were all the same.*

When John Stegall came into his office early in the morning and reached to turn on the lights, a voice said, "Don't! Don't turn on the light!" He was startled and jumped; a figure, a man, was sitting on the corduroy couch against the wall. He was in shadows. Stegall tensed. Eloise was not yet at her desk, so the person must have let himself in.

"All right," Stegall said. "Why?" He squinted at the man. He seemed to be old, with a gray beard. His clothes were dark and, as far as John could see, rather formal. "Whoever you are, I need the light to see," Stegall said. "How did you get in here?"

"I drifted through the wall," the man said.

"Pardon me? You did what?"

"I don't need a door. Locks mean nothing to me. I am of the air. I am a spirit."

"Posh," Stegall said, flipping on the light. "You look real enough to me." The man had bushy gray hair that looked sleep-mussed, a gray beard, and he wore old fashioned clothes that looked—Stegall flashed back in his mind—very like the costumes in the recent college production of *A Doll's House* on campus. A dark gray waistcoat and vest, black pants. (The president had found the play difficult to follow and had dozed through most of it; he had to admit, however, that that Miss Putnam was very easy on the eyes.) Stegall noted that the man wore penny loafers, totally incongruous with the rest of his dress. "Who the hell are you?" Stegall asked. "Pardon my French," he added.

"I am Thomas Waverly Ferguson," the man said. Thomas Waverly Ferguson had been the first president of Florida Girls' Industrial School; he had been dead fifty years. Or more. John was not sure. He was the man for whom Ferguson Hall was named. The building where that slop-bucket Jefferson had his office.

"The hell you say," Stegall said. "Who are you?"

"I told you. I'm here to confer with you. To give you advice from the other side."

"The other side of what?! Get out of my office. I have a secret button here under the carpet"—Stegall stomped his foot—"that will alert security immediately."

"No, you don't," the man said. "Listen to me. I'm your friend. We have both served as president of this institution. I came before you. I know things that you don't know."

"Whoever you are…" Stegall began.

"I am Thomas Waverly Ferguson," the man interrupted.

"All right, *'Thomas Waverly Ferguson,'*" Stegall said, "Get your butt out of my office. Pardon my…" He stopped.

"You should not speak with profanity to me," the man said, "I was a minister of the gospel." His beard tremored around his mouth. It seemed to be catty-wampus on his face.

"You don't sound like any minister of any gospel," the president said. "And your beard is about to give in to gravity!" The man's voice was ringing a bell. It was a deep southern drawl done with a definite above-the-Mason/Dixon tone. Who it was popped into Stegall's head. Of course. One of those Harmon vermin. And it was easy to hear which one. "You are Donald Katz," Stegall said, "aren't you?"

"No," he said, "I am Thomas Waverly…"

"Remove yourself from my office, Dr. Katz, or I will call security and have you arrested."

Just then Eloise stuck her head in the door. "John?" she said, "who are you talking to?" She came on into the office and stopped short when she spotted the man on the sofa. She narrowed her eyes, inspecting his garb. "Who…who is this?" she said. "I mean…Mr. Uh…Mr…I don't believe we've been introduced."

"He was just leaving, Eloise," Stegall said. "This is Dr. Katz, from the biology department."

"Dr. Katz?!" she questioned.

"Yes. He 'got himself up' this morning. A childish prank. Just what you'd expect from Harmon Hall."

"Well, I…I don't understand," Mrs. Hoyle said.

"Good-bye, Dr. Katz," Stegall said, "have a good day."

Katz stood up. He straightened his beard on his face. He looked fiercely at Mrs. Hoyle. "I am Thomas Waverly Ferguson," he said.

"Well, I never," Eloise said.

Katz moved stiffly toward the door. He paused, looking at them once more. "I must retire to my casket," he said, "where I rest for eternity! But I shall return."

"Return to Harmon Hall, you mountebank," Stegall said. He laughed. "Next time come up with something more clever!"

Katz exited the office. They heard him move through the outer office, through the foyer, and then out the front door. It slammed to behind him.

"Those people are trying to drive me crazy," Stegall said to Eloise, "but I won't let them get away with it. No sir! That inflated blimp Jefferson is behind this! I know it! But I'm too smart for them!"

"Yes sir," Eloise said.

"I want that son-of-a...son-of-a-gun in my office, Eloise. But first I need to think on it. I'll let you know when I want him summoned!"

"Yes sir," she said. "You have an appointment this morning at nine with Richard Smart. (Smart was the current president of the faculty senate.) Don't forget to pump up your chair."

"Yes, Eloise, thank you," he said. He began to push the lever as she left his office.

CHAPTER THIRTEEN

Lily and Charles Stewart were sitting off-stage in the auditorium/ large classroom in Comer Hall, waiting for the beginning of his seminar/discussion group with students. His lecture the previous evening, in Lily's estimation, had been absolutely brilliant; he had focused mostly on "Among School Children," and Lily had hung onto every word. She had sat by Brass and had been enchanted with the entire lecture. She felt lucky to be exposed to such an accomplished and gifted man. And his expertise, his delivery, was a powerful aphrodisiac to her. She fidgeted in the chair next to him. She felt his dynamism in the air between them.

Lillian Lallo, in her role as co-chair of the Yancey Committee, had introduced Dr. Stewart last night. She had gone on and on, being so personal that one would have thought she had known Charles Stewart all her life rather than having just met him. Lily sensed that the woman was as turned on by their visitor as she was; she was amused. Tight little Lillian was unctuous in the extreme.

"I think she has Charlie confused with Jesus Christ," Lily whispered to Brass, and Brass had chortled with his hand over his mouth.

Now Charles Stewart said to her, in a tone that Lily thought was somewhat proprietary, "Why didn't you come to the apartment last night after the lecture?"

"Well," she said, "I didn't know I was invited."

"Of course you were invited! I had to sit in that place—that smells, by the way, of Pine-sol—and drink myself to sleep all by myself. My sheets were too chilly."

"If you had asked me, I might have come," she said. "I had preparations to do, but I probably would have come over later. I can't read your mind."

"Oh, no? What am I thinking of right now?" He gave her a simmering look.

"Good god, Charlie," she said, "you're fixing to go in there and talk to students, and your mind is in the place of excrement!"

"Lovely allusion to Crazy Jane," he said, "and your charming southern 'fixing to' fills my member with hot blood."

"Charlie! Shhh, they'll overhear."

"I'm not kidding you. You have that effect on me," he said.

"I have that effect on a lot of men, unfortunately," she said.

"Unfortunately? Whatever do you mean?"

"I get very weary of fending off guys who don't want to do anything but get in my panties."

"Can you blame them? You are luscious and heavenly, my dear. Don't say panties again, or I won't be able to walk out there without embarrassing myself."

"Something tells me," she said, "that you wouldn't be very embarrassed at all. You probably want all the little coeds to swoon over your bulging 'member,' as you call it."

"It is bulging, all right," Stewart said.

"Let's get off this, Charlie," she said. "It's almost time. Is there anything more you want me to say in my introduction, other than all that Dr. Lallo said last night?"

"That woman was creaming her panties. Oops, there I go again. Panties." He panted theatrically. "Don't say all that shit, okay? They can read the fucking program. Just say, 'Heere's Charlie!'"

"Okay," she said, relieved. "I won't say much more than that."

"Just say 'Here's the man I'm going to fuck in an hour!'"

"Shhh! An hour? I have a class. Life goes on, Charlie, even though you're here."

"Oh, I know, dear one." He smiled at her. "Afternoon delight, then?"

"We'll see," she said.

Brasfield Finch stopped off at Stache's on his way home to have a dry Martini. The early spring weather was temperate, the sky clear blue, and he had walked to his office in Comer that morning from his apartment across town. *I must do this more frequently,* he thought, *good for the old legs.* He had not driven his old beat-up Ford sedan that day, the same one that Lily had expressed doubts about the previous spring when Finch had driven her into Tallahassee to meet Lenora Hart.

"Will this thing get us there?" she'd asked, looking it over.

"Yes mam," he'd said, opening the door for her with a sweeping blandishment, as though it were a golden carriage. "She'll not only get us there, but get us there in style. This old girl has two hundred and sixty thousand miles on her, and she runs like a sewing machine!"

"She?" Lily had said. "I thought Ford was masculine."

"Not my baby," he had said. Finch thought his car was fully in keeping with his mode of dress, with the complete picture that he presented to the world.

He now relaxed with his cocktail; the bartender at Stache's, a heavy-set girl name Miriam Wesley, who was one of Finch's former students—not a very good fiction writer but a marvelous bartender—made an exceptional Martini. He looked around the room; it was early and many of the tables were empty. With a jolt he spotted him, alone at a table in the corner: Rudolph Cowan. He had changed from his madras to all khaki, with a work shirt very like one Finch might himself have worn. Cowan sat with an empty beer glass on the table in front of him, leveling his gaze at Finch. He was not staring; he was glaring. *What is up with this fellow?* Finch thought nervously. *I had nothing to do with his escapade; I hardly knew him.* Cowan *had* come to Finch's apartment once, with the rest of the class, for shrimp and beer; he had been taciturn, just as he usually was in class, sitting in a corner nursing a beer and, Finch recalled, refusing to eat the shrimp.

"They are nothing more than living sewer pipes," he had said, much to the amusement of the other students. He had eaten lots of crab dip—that Finch had bought in a deli in Tallahassee, along with the fresh steamed shrimp—and crackers.

"I see you don't have any issue with crabs, though?" Finch had asked him.

"Is that what this is?" the boy had asked, his mouth full.

After a few minutes Cowan got up and walked over to Finch's table. He stood there, his eyes narrowed, gazing down at Finch.

"Good afternoon, Mr. Cowan," Finch said. "How are you?"

"Not fine and dandy," he said.

"Oh, well I'm sorry to hear that," Brasfield said, "what can I do to make your life better?"

"Don't shit me, Finch," Cowan said. Finch *had* been shitting him; now he wished he'd just kept his mouth shut. He couldn't stop himself from rattling on.

"You *don't* seem to be in a very good mood, Mr. Cowan," Finch said.

"Would you be if you was me?" the man said.

"I'm sure I don't know, since I'm *not* you."

"No, you're sure not me," Cowan said. He just stood there, passively contemplating Finch, as though he were inspecting him. Finch remembered the man's fondness for long pauses, so he sipped his icy Martini and waited. Finally, he said,

"Would you like to sit down, Mr. Cowan?"

Cowan sat down at the table. Finch decided to be bold. "Do we have to fear you, Mr. Cowan?" he asked.

"What do you mean?"

"Well, you vowed revenge, if I recall correctly."

"Maybe," he said, "maybe not."

"Would you like another beer? I could get Randy…"

"No! I'm not supposed to have even one, but it sure was good. So nice and cold and good."

"I'm sure it was," Finch said. "I'd be happy to buy you another one."

"No way, man. Okay?" He seemed to relax a bit in the stiff wooden chair. "Okay?" he said again.

"Of course," Finch said. The boy made Finch edgy, ill at ease. It was the look in his eyes. They didn't seem quite focused, yet they bore into Finch like a laser beam. "How are you getting on?" asked Finch. "Now that you're...out?"

"I'm on my way to Dallas," Cowan said.

"Dallas? What's in Dallas?" *Why can't I keep my fucking mouth shut?*

"It's a city," Cowan said.

"I guess you have family there." *Shut the fuck up!* "Not that it's any of my business, Rudy," he added. He had all of a sudden, without warning, recalled that the other students called the man Rudy when he was in school.

"No, it's not," Rudy said. "My grandmother."

"Oh? That's nice." *The creature has a grandmother? How am I going to deal with this man? How to get rid of him? I want another Martini.* "Are you sure you won't..."

"Yes, I'm sure. They told me I couldn't drink alcohol. It'll make me do bad things. I don't really want to do bad things. That's why I'm going to Dallas."

"Of course. Yes," said Finch. *Dallas? Just sit here, keep your mouth shut.* "Flying, I suppose?" Finch asked. He waved in the air for Randy. He could have kicked himself under the table. *Why am I encouraging this insane murderer to talk?*

"No," Cowan said, "walking." He laughed. He grinned. His teeth were crooked and yellow. He bellowed, as though he thought what he'd said was extremely funny. Finch made himself chuckle.

Just then Randy arrived at the table. He wore a stained white apron, his pony tail disheveled down his back. "What you need?" he said. "Rudy? Another dry for Mr. Finch, coming up."

"Nothing for me, thanks," Cowan said. "I won't even drink your water, because you put poison in it. Give your poison to Finch, not me. I must leave for Dallas." When Randy went back behind the bar, Cowan stood up. He leaned forward, both hands on the table. His eyes looked hot and curiously amused. They glinted. "Farewell, Finch," he said, "if you ever get to Dallas, watch your back." He turned and went out the side door, toward the parking lot.

When Randy brought his fresh Martini, Finch said, "Randy, that man is bonkers."

"If that's an old fashioned way of saying he's shit-brained, yes sir," Randy said.

When Charles Stewart showed up for his second scheduled seminar with students—fifteen minutes late—Lily knew immediately that he'd been drinking. He had a crooked smile on his face as though he were inwardly amused. He looked pleasantly preoccupied; his tie was twisted and aslant on his chest as if he had hastily knotted it. "Yes, yes," he said, standing, when Lily introduced him. "Ask me anything," he said. He grinned at the students. "Don't be afraid," he said, "fire away." He had made no remarks, had no notes or book, and Lily knew she'd need to jump-start the situation. She pointed to one of her students.

"Mr. Shannarah," she said, "I think you had a question for Dr. Stewart."

"Yes mam," he said. "Yeats wrote his own epitaph. To quote: 'Cast a cold eye/On life, on death/Horseman, pass by.' What did he mean by that?"

"What do you mean, what did he mean by it?" Stewart said. It was ten in the morning, and his tongue was thick.

"I mean," Bobby Shannarah said, "who is the horseman?"

"*You* are the horseman!" Stewart said. "Everybody is the horseman, the fu…(he caught himself)..freaking *world* is the horseman." He leaned on the lectern. "You all must understand that his epitaph is the last bit of his poem 'Under Ben Bulben,' and Yeats felt that this was the last thing he would say on earth. Of course it wasn't. During his last illness, he probably said 'wipe my ass' or something. Ha ha ha." The students roared with laughter. They *liked* this guy from Harvard, though few of them understood much of what he told them. She knew her own students had read "Among School Children"; at least she had assigned it and discussed it with them. She had no idea about the others. Willow had not seemed overly impressed with his visit. "He's okay, Lily," she'd said, refusing to comment further on his lecture, "go for it! I suppose he's good for *that*."

"Ben Bulben is a mountain near Yeats' grave," Stewart continued, "it is a sacred place in Ireland. Ireland reveres its poets, unlike America. We revere only bull-headed athletes, movie and TV stars and awful Grammy winners! America does not revere its poets!"

"What about Robert Frost?" a girl—not one of Lily's students—asked.

"What about him?" Stewart said. There was no response forthcoming from the audience. Stewart chortled. He seemed to be perspiring. "Okay, exception. People *love* Robert Frost. He is the kindly old gray haired New England uncle that all of us wish we had, always stopping by woods on a snowy evening and such, except that he wasn't kindly. He was a mean son-of-a-bitch who didn't mind plowing another man's pasture, if you get what I mean. Robert Frost! People love the idea of Robert Frost, but they don't have the foggiest understanding of his poems. They get them all wrong! (Lily recalled the day in the Yancey Committee meeting way last fall when Dean Wallace Jefferson had made a comment that indicated he had no clue about the line "good fences make good neighbors.") But all right," Stewart went on, "Robert Frost is the poet hero! He and Rod McKuen. Rod McKuen. Ugh! But there are other poets: What about John Berryman? What about William Meredith? Aha! Never heard of them, have you? But they are finer poets than Robert Frost, or Rod McKuen. Ugh! And America does not revere them. When they die, will there be a Ben Bulben for them to repose under? I doubt it. You can go to the Cathedral of St. John the Divine in Manhattan and look at the poets' window, the poets' corner, but how many people do that? Go to the Cathedral of St. John the Divine and you will find mostly winos and street people who wouldn't know a poet if one jumped up and bit them on the ass." (More raucous laughter; if you want to get a group of undergraduate college students going, just throw in a few mild expletives. They are *hearing* what you say, but they are not *listening* to what you say.)

Lily looked out over the gathering. She could see Brass Finch on the back row. His face was neutral. She could well imagine how all this talk of poets was sitting with him. She looked at Bobby Shannarah, her student. He was frowning. Lily surmised that he thought that Stewart had not answered his question. Bobby was dark and handsome, though slight; his parents were Palestinian immigrants who worked as shrimpers out of Destin. Lily liked him. "Did you answer Mr. Shannarah's question?" she asked Stewart when he paused.

"Who is this Mr. Shannarah?" Stewart asked.

Lily sighed. "The student who asked you the question about Yeats' epitaph," she said.

"Oh yes! I answered that question. I answered it voluminously. It means whatever Mr. Shannarah thinks it means. Yeats is not going to pop up out of his grave and *explain* to you what he meant. Either you get it or you don't. Next question." Smiling, he pointed to a very pretty coed sitting on the second row with her hand up.

"Was Yeats gay?" she asked.

"Why do you ask that?" Stewart said.

"Well, lots of poets are gay." He stared at her as though he couldn't believe what she was saying. He smacked his lips. He shook his head. Finally, he said,

"I doubt that he was gay, Miss…uh…what is your name?"

Uh oh, Lily thought. *A fresh afternoon delight?*

"Martha Posner," she said.

"I doubt it very much, Miss Posner, and thank you for your question. (Miss Posner was beaming.) Yeats was known to diddle a few women (Laughter) and he was married. Of course today we know that doesn't mean a whole lot, but in Yeats' time there was never any suggestion that he was anything but straight. He had two children. Some of his early photographs look a little fey, but he was just looking like a poet. Wavy blonde hair, thick glasses. A nerd to his schoolmates. Does that answer your question, Miss Posner, dear?"

"Yes sir," she said, with a heated smile. She was a goner.

When the seminar was over, Martha Posner came down front. She wanted Stewart "to clarify something." Lily couldn't hear what they were whispering about, their heads together.

After the students were gone, she was walking Charlie back over to Hill House.

"I know the way," he said.

"I know you do," Lily said, "but I'm your host. Your protector."

"Oh? What do you protect me from?"

"I *would* say from horny little coeds, but I fear it's too late for that."

He laughed good-naturedly. "You have the lay of the land, captain," he said. "Listen. I have the rest of the day and tomorrow off before I have to perform again. I'm going to take a long nap this afternoon…"

"Hah!" she said.

"…and I want you over here at five. We'll have a drink. And bring your bikini. We're going to the beach."

"What? The beach?"

"Hell yeah. We'll spend tomorrow looking at the waves and drinking beer. Among other activities." He smiled.

"I have a class tomorrow, Charlie," she said.

"Cut it. Dismiss them. Come on…'I will arise and go now'… all that shit! I *command* you. 'Where peace comes dropping slow!' I will not take no for an answer."

She hesitated for only a moment. "Okay, Charlie," she said. *What the hell?* Brass or Willow could dismiss her class. No problem. She could use a day at the beach.

"Be here at five," he said. "I have a rental car and a reservation at a condo on West Panama City Beach. I'll have a thermos full of dry Martinis. We can drive down before dinner. Fresh oysters on the half shell. Puts iron in your blood. Don't be late."

"Okay, Charlie, I won't," she said.

Walking back over to her office, she found herself looking forward to the beach. But not so much with him. She was getting a little weary of the man, the way he ordered her around. Ordered *everybody* around. Maybe she should just tell him that she couldn't dismiss her class and could not go. But she knew she would not do that. She would go. She would let him order her to go, but it did not register well in her psyche. She had enjoyed the sex with him, two afternoon delights and two late night trysts. But the man was carrying a tremendous load of garbage, and she would not let him dump any of it on her. He was not truthful. He had said he would not drink before meeting with students, but he had been drinking before ten in the morning. She smelled it on him; she could tell by the way he pronounced his words very precisely, as though he had to think about them before he uttered them. Was he a phony? He was a brilliant man who made Yeats' poetry come alive. A compelling writer about the poet's work. But from the way he conducted his seminar, she discerned that he cared little about the students and their questions. Was he one of those ivory tower scholars she'd always heard about? Lily was a teacher, and she respected teaching. She was proud of herself for being in the trenches, but she was bothered by Stewart's seeming contempt for everything connected to Lakewood College, its students, and its mission. He was a cynic, a drunk and a womanizer. *Then why in the hell am I going off to the beach with this man?*

She arrived at Hill House at ten minutes after five. She saw, in the near distance, down the brick sidewalk, the figure of Martha Posner walking back to her dorm. *Just like I'm a little late on purpose; maybe he held her back because he wanted me to see her.* He opened the door to her knock; he had a drink in a clear plastic cup. He wore navy Bermuda shorts, leather sandals, and a pink polo shirt; he had on aviator sunglasses. He had apparently come prepared. He held his drink up to her.

"Not the best Martini glasses," he said, "these were all I could find in the kitchen. They look like punch cups. But they'll do, won't they. What's that?" he said, indicating her Harvard book bag.

"It's my overnight case," she said. She did not have a regular one, so she'd dumped the papers and books out and put in her bikini, fresh lingerie, a change of blouse and shorts, her toothbrush and paste, and a lipstick, which was all the makeup she used, and not much of that.

"Never seen one quite like that," he said. He had packed a little leather satchel that was sitting on the floor by the front door.

"Actually," she said, "it's my Harvard book bag."

"Your Harvard *what*?!"

"My Harvard book bag."

He whistled between clenched teeth, picking up his valise. "Never saw anything like that in my life," he said. "Certainly not at Harvard. Let's go."

He walked behind her on the way to the car, and she knew he was appreciating her butt in her tight white shorts. She said, over her shoulder,

"In graduate school, everybody called them Harvard book bags."

"Huh," he said, opening the door. "Get in. Throw your *Harvard* book bag in the back seat."

He sped down the brick street to the campus gate and came to a grinding halt. "Where do I go from here?" he asked.

"Straight ahead. We'll turn left up here at Highway sixty nine."

"How utterly delightful!" he said. "Sixty nine with sweet Lily! At the beach! What could be more wonderful?"

They got under way, both sipping their drinks. She wondered how much he'd been drinking this afternoon. He drove fast, passing cars on the two lane road. Highway sixty nine would take them directly into Panama City Beach. They passed a sign: BEACHES, 35 miles. "Shit, I didn't know it was that far," he said. He pressed the accelerator down further.

"Hey, Charlie," she said, "why don't you let me drive? You're going to kill us!"

"Hell no," he said, "no woman is driving me anywhere. And you've been drinking!"

"What about you, motherfucker?!" she said, gripping the oh-shit bar. "Look out!"

He was coming up too fast on an old truck that was puttering down the road. The truck carried a huge roll of hay on its bed, weighing it down. Stewart slammed on the brakes.

"Goddammit," he said.

"Slow down, Charlie," she said, "or I swear there'll be no sixty nine or anything else at the beach!"

"Okay, okay," he said. He seemed to suddenly relax. He leaned back against the seat, following the truck. He had spilled most of his Martini on his leg, and he tossed off what remained. He handed her his plastic glass. "Hit me again," he said. "Wonderful Martinis, fantastic day...we'll get there in time to see the sunset." He was wiping away at his leg with his bare hand. "I guess there are worse things to smell like than Martinis," he said. He let go with a belly laugh. "Fine time, Lily girl! Beach, here we come!"

He passed the old truck. The hay almost brushed Lily's side of the rental car, and she tensed as she saw a car coming around a curve toward them. He whipped the car back into the right lane quickly, and the man in the truck blew his horn at them.

"Blow it out of your ass, brother!" he shouted. The road was now flat and straight, with tall pines set back on both sides. The ditches were sandy. They began to pass sparse palm trees and palmettos. Lily was aware when they crossed the salt line; she breathed deeply of the air. They passed mobile homes with exploding bursts of red azaleas in the front yards. They passed a dog track.

"Just a few more miles," Lily said.

Finally they passed another sign: WELCOME TO PANAMA CITY BEACH. As they were approaching the intersection of sixty nine and U. S. highway ninety eight, he slowed.

"This place is called Pinnacle Point," he said. "You know where it is? Or I can stop and get directions."

"Sure," she said, "I've stayed there before. And it's Pinnacle *Port*, not point. Turn right up here."

They stood on the balcony overlooking the blue-green Gulf; the sun was setting, the sky colored with salmon and apricot against the high clouds. "Fan-fucking-tastic," Stewart said.

"Yes, it's glorious," Lily said. They sat in the Adirondack chairs on the balcony and put their sandaled feet up on the railing.

"Now this is living," he said, as the fresh sea breezes washed over them. "We should just stay here. Forever."

"What about your classes at Harvard?" she said. She laughed.

"Fuck my classes at Harvard," he said. "How long have you known about this?"

"What?"

"This beach! All that white, white sand. In New England the sand is baby-shit brown! And those streaks of emerald in the water. This is amazing! Why do they keep it a secret?"

She couldn't stop laughing. Finally she said, "It's *not* a secret, Charlie! People from all over the south come here. It's the redneck Riviera. You should see it at Spring Break. Kids from all over the country. The beach is packed and the beer flows."

"Really?"

"Yes, really," she said. "No locals come down here then; it's a mad-house."

"Really?" he said again. "Probably lots of young pussy on the beach." He sighed. He was on what she thought was his fourth, maybe his fifth, Martini since they had left Lakewood. He shook his head. "Wonders never cease," he said. After a few minutes he said, "Let's go to dinner. Where shall we go?"

She took him to a place called Dusty's, on Front Beach Road;

she prevailed on him to let her drive, ostensibly so he could get a better look at the beach. He agreed, after some resistance. He seemed happy to be able to sit back and drink his Martini. He kept muttering, "Fantastic," and "Terrific." At Dusty's he drank three Bud Lights and ate three dozen raw oysters on the half shell and half a pound of steamed shrimp. He lathered them all with horseradish. Lily had had a half dozen baked oysters and grilled grouper, and he liked the looks of the grouper and had a taste of hers, so he ordered blackened grouper and devoured it hungrily, along with the cole slaw and French fries that came with it. On the way home he dozed off in the passenger seat. When she parked in front of their building, she poked him on the arm. He didn't move. She poked him again and pinched his arm.

"Listen to me, asshole," she said in his ear. "If you don't wake up I'm going to leave you right here." He still didn't respond. "And let the crabs get you," she said.

His eyes popped open. He blinked. He looked at her with astonishment. "They can get in the car?!" he asked.

She shoved him again. "Come on, get out. You have to walk in. I can't carry your ass." He started stirring. "Or I can call security," she said.

"No, no," he mumbled. He struggled out. "Shit," he said. She had to support him on rubbery legs as they walked to the elevator and went up to their floor. "Shouldn't have had that last beer," he grunted as they entered their condo. She chuckled. She led him into the bedroom, where he fell fully clothed on the bed and was passed out before she could leave the room.

They had left the door open with the screen closed, and when Lily went back into the living room she could hear the waves bursting on the shore; the air that wafted through the screen was cool and damp. *There is a squall coming in from out in the Gulf,* she thought. *Good sleeping tonight.* Lily rummaged around in the small kitchen and found a bottle of tonic; she made herself a gin and tonic and took it out to the balcony. The breeze was invigorating; it energized her. There was lightening on the horizon, and she could hear distant rumbles of thunder. She was not tired, but the waves would rock her to sleep as if she were an infant.

She was relieved that the son-of-a-bitch was passed out. *How did I get to be his keeper and his vessel?* Of course, she had asked for it. *I was too easy*, she thought, *sometimes I'm too easy*. At times Stewart reminded her a little bit of Brass, but Brass did not have that hard cynical edge. He was more laid back, about everything. Even after they'd slept together, Brass had never once acted proprietary toward her. He wanted her to be her own woman, not to be some extension of a man. He encouraged her to flower. Charlie Stewart was just the opposite; his actions and sometimes his words told her that as far as he was concerned, she was *his toy* for the week, even to instructing her to leave him alone to fuck a young girl who might not even be of legal age. She doubted that he cared. He was a narcissist, through and through.

When she went to bed, she pushed him as far as she could to the edge of the bed so she could get the spread and the sheet down. Lily slept nude; that's how she was comfortable. She lay with the sheet over her, listening to the waves. Then she drifted off.

The next morning he was still snoring softly, his polo shirt twisted around his neck. Lily smiled. He was probably as uncomfortable as hell. She put on her bikini, a bright red one, and went out and made coffee. She took her cup out to the balcony. It was going to be another gorgeous day. She drank several cups of coffee, then ate a dough-nut from a dozen that he had insisted on buying when they had stopped at a roadside food-mart.

She went down to the beach, leaving him asleep. She sat down in a padded beach chair and adjusted the umbrella to get the morning sun on her legs. A beach-boy appeared. "I'm Max," he said. "These chairs are twenty bucks a day." His eyes were bulging out of his head. He couldn't refrain from gaping at her.

"Put it on Dr. Charles Stewart's bill, Max," she said, "and bring me a Bloody Mary when you get a chance. Extra hot. Put that on his bill, too." She smiled at the helpless boy. He stood there, as if he couldn't tear himself away. "Come on, buddy boy," she said, "Vamos! I need my BM." His mouth fell open. "*Bloody Mary*! Make it a double." She giggled when he trudged away in the sand.

She had another drink while she was relaxing in the sun. She was placid and easy when she went back up to the condo. Stewart was up, sitting on the sofa with a cup of coffee. "Morning, sunshine," she said. "How's your head?"

He glared at her, his eyes narrowed. He looked her up and down. "Shit!" he said. He shook his head. After a minute he said, "Don't tell me you went down to the beach looking like that!"

"Like what?" she asked, shocked. "I've just got on my bikini. What are you talking about?"

"It's a *string* bikini," he said, "almost a thong. You're practically naked. And the top doesn't fit. Your tits are hanging out!"

"Whoa, here," she said. "What the hell do you mean? Are you telling me that you don't *approve* of my choice of swim wear?"

"That's exactly what I'm saying."

"Well, fuck you, then," she said.

"*I* brought you down here. *I* get to see you naked. Not every fucking man on the beach!"

"Who do you think you are, Charlie?! You think you *own* me?"

"While we're here, yes!"

"Well, think again, buster brown! Nobody owns me, especially some alcoholic brainy who thinks he's God's gift to the world! You better just revise your thinking, buddy boy!"

"Oh shit," he said, rubbing his forehead. He lay down on the couch. "I'm in bad shape. I vomited when I got up."

"Really?" she said, "I see the puke dribbled on your shirt. Completes the picture. I hope you brought a clean one."

He moaned. "Make me a Martini," he said.

"Jesus, Charlie," she said, "wouldn't you rather have a Bloody Mary? I can order you one up from the tiki-hut."

"No. Martini. Hair of the dog."

"I'm not your fucking bartender, but I'll make you one," she said. "Want a dough-nut?"

He groaned. He had his hand over his eyes. "Get me a wet washcloth from the bathroom, will you?" he asked.

"I'm not your servant, either, but I'll do that for you, too," she said.

When she came back with his Martini he sat up and gulped it. "Another," he said.

"Jesus Christ, friend, you *are* in bad shape. But don't worry. I'll drive us home, after I change out of my *scandalous* bikini."

"But we haven't…" He paused. He seemed to be feeling better. The gin was fueling him.

"No, we haven't," she said. "And I don't think we will. You need to get home and sober up. You have two more lectures to give. And I have work to do. Classes. You'll never hear me say 'fuck my classes.'"

"Who would say such a thing?" he asked.

"Oh my Lord, Charlie," she said, chortling, "just drink your gin and I'll get us back to Lakewood."

He spent the rest of the morning lying on the sofa with the rag over his eyes, periodically sipping gin. She ordered another Bloody Mary and a hamburger from the tiki-hut, and the boy brought it up to their room. She got out Charlie's wallet and tipped the boy twenty bucks.

"Hey, thanks," he said, his eyes as round as a salad plate. His blonde hair was sun-bleached and shaggy; he wore baggy shorts and flip-flops.

"Don't spend it all in one place, Max" she said. "Oh, wait a minute. Here." She gave him two more of Charlie's twenties.

"Sixty bucks for a tip?" he said. He was cute. She kissed him on the cheek. "When I call you in a little while, I want you to help me take this sack of shit down to the car," she said, indicating the sprawled figure on the couch.

Around noon, Stewart sat up and said, "I'm feeling better."

"You're drunk, Charlie," she said.

She called Max and the two of them struggled out with Stewart, whose legs seemed useless, as if he had forgotten how to use them. She was afraid he would throw up again, this time all over them. He didn't. They got him into the back seat and Lily drove back to Lakewood. She parked the car in the lot behind Hill House and left him sleeping there.

On the evening after Stewart's fourth and final lecture, he and Lily were lying naked on the double bed in the Hill House apartment. They had just made love for the fifth time that week, a regularity interrupted only by their trip to the beach. Stewart was a licentious lover, but even though he was usually drunk he was inexplicably inhibited. He walled off from Lily. He seemed to have trouble relating to her as a woman, as another person, just as, Lily suspected, he was to everybody else. He continued to drink heavily and he would freeze up in moments when she softened and tried to make herself especially close to him. As soon as they were done physically, he withdrew; he was not emotionally available. Their romp had started out to be fun. Now it was almost a chore for her. She would be glad when he was gone. She hated that part of herself that continued to want to sleep with him; her other half wanted nothing to do with him. He was a misogynist, a narcissist, and a cynic. She did not like him. Now he said, smoking a cigarette as they lay there in bed, "That man who introduced me tonight. The Dean. He could play Falstaff!"

"He'd be perfect if he had the sense of humor for the part," she said. "He's certainly fat enough."

They watched his smoke drift up to the ceiling. "I didn't particularly like the introduction last night, though," he said. It had been Rufus Doublet, their erstwhile department chair. "I thought *he* was going to cream his jeans. That guy's as queer as a dodo bird."

"That's not politically correct, 'queer,'" she said.

"Fuck political correctness," he said, "a fag is a fag."

"Well, I have to say I agree with the gist of what you're saying, I just don't especially like the way you're saying it."

"What are you, Lily? Some bleeding heart? Some pseudo feminist?"

"I'm not 'pseudo' anything," Lily said. "I just don't like putting people down because they are different from me."

"God, woman, don't you know that a fag is just a guy who corn-holed his buddy when they were adolescents and never got over it? I corn-holed my buddy, but I got over it. I got over it quick! I like women!"

"But you fucked *me* in the ass," Lily said.

"That's different. You're a woman. And a hell of a woman! I have used every hole on you, with the exception of your nostrils and your ears, and that's the way of things. That's what god intended."

"God? What the hell are you talking about?" He didn't answer, just took another drag off his cigarette. "You're a fucking Mormon," she said accusingly.

"Who told you that?" he snapped.

"Nobody told me. I read it in your bio."

"My bio says nothing about my religious beliefs today. It only says I was raised in the Mormon Church." He jammed his cigarette out and sat up in bed. The black hair on his chest was kinky and curled away under the sheet at his waist. He kicked the sheet away. He had an erection. "Turn over," he said, "I'm coming in."

"No hell you're not," Lily said. She pulled the sheet up to her neck. "I don't know who you think you are, Charlie, but you're not coming in! I've about had it with you!"

He gripped her shoulder. Hard. "I said turn over on your stomach, hike it up here. I'm not going to tell you again."

"*Tell* me? No!" Her shoulder was turning red where he clutched her. "Let me go. You're hurting me!" She struggled away from him; he grabbed her with both hands. He forced her down on the bed, holding both her wrists in an iron grip with one of his hands. He was far stronger than she was. "I'll scream!" she said. He ripped the sheet away from her and tossed it to the floor. "Help..." she started to scream, and he clamped his hand over her mouth.

"Shut up, woman!" he said. He was on top of her, fumbling. She tried to keep her legs squeezed. His solid knee pushed brutally between her thighs. She felt his penis forcing its way in. Thank goodness she was still creamy from their earlier action. He huffed. He panted. "My God, woman," he grunted, "you fuck like an animal!"

"Unh, unh," she said, twisting her face beneath his hand. She got her mouth open. She chomped down on the tender flesh at the base of his palm. She bit as hard as she could.

"Jesus fucking Christ!" he said, jerking his hand away. It was bleeding. "You bitch!" he said. He drew back his other hand in a fist.

"Go ahead," she said, "hit me, you asshole." He stopped moving. He just stared down at her. "Hit me, you fucking Mormon," she said.

He seemed frozen for a moment, his fist raised. She looked into his eyes; she saw a bewildered, turbulent turmoil there. His eyes seemed focused somewhere far away, as though he didn't even know who she was. He crumbled on top of her and rolled over; he was weeping, tears running down his face. He sobbed, drawing his breath with sharp intakes. His eyes were now shut tight, squeezing the tears out.

"Charlie," she said, gently, comfortingly. "Charlie, take it easy." She rested her palm on his forehead. It seemed hot to the touch. She slid over and cradled his head in the crook of her arm. "Charlie," she whispered. They lay in that bizarre embrace for a long time. Until Lily arose, dressed, and made her way back to her apartment.

CHAPTER FOURTEEN

When President John W. Stegall arrived at his office on this splendid, exquisite spring day, Eloise Hoyle, already at her desk, greeted him heartily and joyfully. "Morning, Prez," she said, "the Lord has given us another glorious day!"

"Good morning, Eloise," he said, "and may you have a blessed day!"

Stegall had walked from Flower Hill to Woodfin Hall, as was his usual habit, greeting students on their way to their eight o'clock classes. He had seen several junior faculty members hastily parking their cars and hastening into their buildings, their faces turned away from him, as though that might make the boss not notice that they were late. Most of the early classes were taught by instructors and junior faculty, but he had seen Willow Behn making her way into Comer Hall, carrying her old worn leather briefcase that she'd probably had since graduate school. He wondered if Willow had an eight o'clock. He would have to have Eloise look it up. He liked to keep check on his faculty. What they were doing and when they were doing it.

Eloise had just watered the plants in his office and he could smell the damp soil. He sat down behind his desk; the day lay before him in all its comforting emptiness. Ah, it was incredibly awesome to be the admiral of the ship and to let the vessel plow through the waters on its own, because he had given it such exceptionally gargantuan leadership and direction. The only fly in the ointment was his grossly rotund dean. *Why didn't that bossy wife of his put him on a diet?* The dean had gotten in league with the Bolsheviks on campus and they were attempting their dirty tricks to cause him a breakdown, or worse, a heart attack, but he was on to them and their

A Good Life

sophomoric tactics. He would turn the tables on them, by damn!

His phone rang and he picked up. "Dr. Stegall," Eloise said, "There is a gentleman here to see you. He says he represents Houghton-Mifflin Book Company."

"I don't see book sellers," Stegall said. "Tell him to go away." He heard Eloise talking to the man. "Tell him to go see professors, they're the ones who buy the books. This fellow must be new."

Eloise came back on. "Sir, he says he is executive vice president of Houghton-Mifflin." Stewart let that bit of information gurgle in his brain. "He says he has traveled down here from New York to discuss with you the possibility of a book project."

"A book project? What the hell does he mean? Pardon my French, Eloise." He heard Eloise murmuring to the man.

"He says they want a memoir from you."

"From me? About what?"

"A memoir, sir. About your life and your tenure as leader of a prominent liberal arts college."

"Is this some kind of joke? Is he one of those cretins from Harmon Hall?"

"I don't think so, sir. I've never seen the gentleman before. Should I show him in?"

Stewart hesitated. "I suppose so," he said.

Eloise ushered the man in. He was not someone Stewart had seen before, yet there was something indistinctly and vaguely familiar about him, as if Stewart had seen a picture of him somewhere long ago and far away. The man was stout, dark, as though he spent a lot of time in the sun. His brownish hair was like a layer of thin felt on his head. He wore a royal blue suit with white plaid markings on it; the lapels were wide and his tie was a large, colorful paisley pattern. The man had on shoes with two-inch heels. Odd. His eyes were like faded olives in his round face. He carried a heavy satchel. The man didn't look like the executive vice president of *anything*, but what did Stewart know about New York fashion? He had worn the same blue pin striped suits for decades. All that fashion ostentatiousness was not for him.

"I am John W. Stegall," the president said, sticking out his hand. He did not rise from his office chair, but he was nonetheless at eye level with his guest.

"I am Phillip Wayne Gillespie," the man said, moving to the side of Stegall's massive desk so he could reach the other man's hand. "As your assistant told you, I am..."

"Sit down!" Stewart said. The man obediently sat in one of the visitors' chairs. He placed his satchel on the floor next to him. "Let's get one thing out of the way," the president said, "did that bunch of imbeciles in Harmon Hall send you here?"

"I beg your pardon?" the man said. He seemed genuinely bewildered.

"Can you show me your credentials?" Stewart said curtly.

Gillespie fumbled in his pocket. "Here is my card," he said, shoving it across the desk. "That should do," he said, a tinge of defensiveness in his voice.

Stewart read it. PHILLIP WAYNE GELLESPIE, EXECUTIVE VICE PRESIDENT, HOUGHTON-MIFFLIN PUBLISHING COMPANY, NEW YORK, NEW YORK. "I'm sorry, Mr. Gillespie," Stewart said, "but you must understand. I have to be very careful. Heavy lies the head that wears a crown. I hope you understand and forgive me."

"Of course," the man said. He squinted at Stewart. "How would you like to go to Dallas?" he asked.

"Excuse me?" Stewart said. "Dallas? Dallas, Texas?"

"You know of another Dallas?"

"I'm not planning on going anywhere, Mr. Gillespie," he said, "I have an institution to run. I am a busy man." He chuckled. He was trying to impress this man who had come seeking a book from him.

"What do you do all day, sit here and beat your meat?" Phillip said. "Or does old Olive Hoyle come in here and give you a blow job?"

"Mr. Gillespie!" Stewart said. "Pardon your French. Whatever are you implying?" It began to dawn on Stewart that this man was not who he said he was after all. Stewart had been right with his first premonition. "I'll not have you use such language in this office, sir, whoever you are!"

"What language, beat your meat? Or blow job?"

"Stop! Stop! You are a vulgarian, and I will not have it. Out of my office, sir!" Stewart's cheeks were flaming.

The man reached down and unzipped the satchel and pulled out what looked to Stewart like a fancy rifle. It looked like something you'd see in a war movie. "I'm not going anywhere," the man said, and grinned.

"Wh…what is that?" Stewart asked.

"What does it look like?"

"It looks like a tommy gun. Put it down." The man was pointing the gun directly at Stewart. "Don't point that thing at me, sir," Stewart said. His voice had gotten pinched and windy.

Mr. Gillespie laughed, a reedy, strident huffing. He continued to stare at Stegall, who squirmed in his desk chair. Finally, he said, "Who else is in the building? Besides old Olive Hoyle and you?"

"I…I really don't think that's any of your business, Mr…uh… Gillespie."

The man cocked his weapon. "*This* makes it my business," he said.

"Yes, sir," Stegall said. "I…I don't know. Olive…uh…Eloise would know. Let me call her in." Stegall reached for the phone.

"Don't touch that!" Gillespie said and Stegall jerked his hand back. "Get up and calmly go to the door and get her in here. And remember, this thing is aimed right at your heart. Just tell her to come in."

Stegall did as he was told. His legs were trembling and his voice was quaking when he said, "Eloise, would you come in here, please?"

"What do you need?" Eloise said when she came through the door. She stopped short when she saw Mr. Gillespie with the weapon. "What…what?" she said.

The man got up and moved over to the corduroy couch; he motioned with the gun for them to sit in the visitors' chairs. "I prefer to sit behind my desk," Stewart said, his voice almost a whisper.

"I don't give a shit what you prefer," the man said, "Sit!" They sat down. "Now, skinny lady, who else is in the building? Upstairs?"

"Well," Mrs. Hoyle said, her voice quivering, "There's Mr. Murphy, the dean of men. He came in earlier. And Alberta Wingate just got here."

"Who is this Alberta person?"

"She is the dean of women. Her office is up…"

"Yes. I want you to go to the phone and call them and tell them to come down here for an important meeting. And no funny business. All right?"

Eloise did as she was told. After a minute they heard Big Hoss's heavy footsteps on the stairs. He and Alberta came into the office.

"What's this important…?" Murphy said. He saw Gillespie with the AK-47. "What the fuck, John?" he blurted.

"Shut up!" Gillespie said. "Against the wall. Both of you."

"Well, I never," said Alberta. They moved with their backs against the wall.

"Be quiet, Alberta. What the fuck, John?" Big Hoss said again.

"We are being held captive by the executive vice president of Houghton-Mifflin Publishing Company," Stewart said in a quavering voice.

"You're shitting me," Hoss said. He was peering intently at Gillespie. After a minute, he said, "Hey! This motherfucker is Rudolph Cowan. Rudolph Cowan!" he repeated.

"Hello again, Dean Murphy," Cowan said. "It's so good to see you again."

"Shit fire!" Big Hoss said.

"This is a hostage situation," Cowan said.

"No shit?!" Murphy said.

"Who is Rudolph Cowan?" Alberta asked.

"*That's* Rudolph Cowan, you dumbbell," Big Hoss said, "what did I just say? Just keep your mouth shut!"

Alberta raised her arms over her head and shrieked. Stegall thought that someone on the quad would hear her. Surely! She continued to scream.

"*Now* you catch on, dumb-ass," Hoss said to her.

"Shut up, woman!" Cowan said. He fired a blast through the ceiling and they all jumped. Bits of white ceiling tile rained down in the room. Someone would certainly have heard that! Alberta whimpered. "I said, be quiet." Cowan paused. "You two get up and go over to the wall and stand with your friends," he said to Stegall and Hoyle. They obeyed. "It'll take them a while to get a SWAT team from Tallahassee, but the state troopers and the Lakewood police department, such as it is, are probably already gathering. Now listen up. You, Big Hoss piece of shit, will be our spokesman. Your president has already shit his pants." Cowan was right. Stegall could smell it, could feel a warm clammy dampness in his underpants. "So okay, here's what I want. Olive, you want to write this down?" Eloise got a pad and a pen from Stegall's desk. Her hands were shaking so badly she could hardly write. "Okay. I want a fully fueled up private jet, with room for five people; you're all going with me. I want the jet stocked with a case of A&W root beer, not just any root beer. I want one of those wholesale boxes of Double Bubble..."

"Bubble gum? What the fuck?" Big Hoss exclaimed.

"Yes! Write it down, Olive! I want a box of Hershey bars with almonds, a box of Reese's Peanut Butter Cups. I want those boxes that the clerks use to stock the counters with."

"Aww, shit," said Big Hoss, "I ain't believing this."

"I'm not finished," Cowan said. "I want a case of Haig & Haig Scotch. I don't drink that horse piss that Finch drinks. And several bottles of club soda. Any kind. That ought to be enough to get us there."

"Ge...get us where?" Stegall stammered.

"My friends, we are going to Cuba!" Cowan said.

"Cuba?!" Stegall said. "Like, Havana, Cuba? I thought…"

"You didn't really think we were going to Dallas, did you?"

"I…I…" stammered Stegall.

"Where'd you get that gun, Rudy?" Hoss said. "They ain't legal! Put it down, immediately, or I call the cops."

Cowan laughed. He said, "This one's legal to me. And it's lethal, too." He continued to chortle at his own joke. "They'll be calling you, soon, shit-for-brains. To try to negotiate this situation. Only there ain't going to be any negotiating. They'll do *exactly* what you tell them to do!"

"Where the hell you think they're going to land a jet plane in Lakewood?" Hoss said, and snorted. "Shit-for-brains," he added.

"Don't make him mad!" Alberta squealed.

"Mad?!" Hoss said. "The son of a bitch is already mad as a hatter!"

"Shut up," Cowan said. "Zip it! And don't you worry about the plane. I got it figured out."

The others began to inch away from Stegall, who stood on the end. The smell was permeating the room. "Jesus," Hoss said and wiped at his nose.

CHAPTER FIFTEEN

Outside a crowd had gathered on the quad. The sound of the gunshots had brought them running from all over the campus. "What's going on?" a student called out to Officer Puckett, who was patrolling the brick street in front of Woodfin Hall.

"Stay back! Stay back!" he shouted, motioning to them. He kept them across the street, well away from the building. "There's a man in there with one of them ass-salt rifles, I seen him through the window! I've done called the state police!" Everyone could then hear a distant siren as a squad car approached. More students and faculty arrived with exclamations of "What the hell?" and, from some students—and from Fred C. Dobbs, who came lumbering up—"What the fuck?! Sounded like gunshots!" They were milling about in the bright sunshine.

The patrol car entered campus and came to a screeching stop in front of Woodfin Hall. The two policemen jumped out and crouched behind the car, their pistols at ready. One of them had a bull-horn. "THROW YOUR WEAPON DOWN AND COME OUT, AND NOBODY WILL GET HURT!" the cop shouted through his bull-horn. There was no response from the building. Turning around to the crowd, which was growing larger by the minute, he yelled, "GET BACK! STAY BACK!" It startled the swelling crowd almost to silence. "BACK UP TO THAT FLAG-POLE! THIS IS A DANGEROUS SITUATION!" Nobody moved.

"What's going on, officer?" somebody shouted.

"NOTHING! GO BACK TO YOUR CLASSROOMS AND DORMS!" Still nobody moved; they were determined not to miss a thing.

Inside the president's office they could clearly hear the policeman's bull-horn.

"They've got you surrounded, Cowan," Big Hoss said.

"Fuck you, shit-for-brains," Cowan said. He looked around. They could hear the excited voices again swelling. It sounded like a mob was forming. Then Cowan said, "Jesus Christ, Stegall, who told you a president's shit don't stink? Something crawled up inside you and died, man! Open that window, let some fresh air in here."

"C...Can't," Eloise Hoyle stammered. "When the building was remodeled they were sealed shut."

"Well, fuck it, then," Cowan said, and fired a quick blast at the window, causing his captives to jump and quake. The window shattered and the squeals and cries from the crowd, now whooping and bleating in alarm and fear, grew louder in the room. The two women had their arms around each other. They and Big Hoss were grouped as far away from President Stegall as they could get and still remain against the wall. Stegall sidled toward them.

"P...please," Alberta said, shrinking from him.

The spurt that Cowan fired was three bullets; one pierced the huge American flag that waved over the quad, one went harmlessly into the air and, along with its twin, fell God knew where, and one hit the metal flagpole itself and ricocheted into the mob and struck Fred C. Dobbs in the left buttock. Dobbs went down with a cry of pain and surprise. Some students gathered around him. "What happened, Dr. Dobbs?" one of them said.

"That son-of-a-bitch shot me in the ass," Dobbs grunted.

"Who?! Who shot you in the ass?"

"Whoever's doing the shooting, dumb-ass," Dobbs answered.

Across campus, Brasfield Finch came out of his office; he met Willow Behn coming out of hers. "What was that?" she said.

"Sounded like gun shots," Finch said.

"I heard it earlier," she said, "I thought it was firecrackers. There's a big crowd gathering on the quad. Is it some sort of holiday?"

"No," Finch said. They went into her office, which had a good view of the quad, and peered out the window. "Damn, something's going on," Finch said.

"What?!" Lily said, arriving breathlessly at Willow's door. "What's going on?"

"We don't know," Willow said.

"Well, let's go and find out," Finch said.

"You want to get into that horde?" Willow asked.

"Hell, yeah," Finch said, "stay here if you want to, Willow. Come on, Lily." He grabbed Lily's hand and pulled her into the hall. "Wait a minute," he said. He ran back into his office and had a good, solid snort of Scotch, then poured himself three inches into his coffee cup. By the time he came back out, holding the cup, Willow was standing with Lily. Willow sniffed the air.

"Well fortified, huh, Mr. Finch?" she said.

"Loaded for bear," he said, "come on, girls." They could hear more sirens, more police cars arriving. "Excitement on campus!" he said, "let's go."

When they arrived at the quad it was almost filled with faculty and students. There was a lot of intoxicating emotion in the air, much commotion. They pushed their way through. They could see a line of police cars in front of Woodfin Hall, along with a gray tank-like truck with SWAT written on the side in blue letters. They ran into Garcia Russo. "What's going on, Russo?" Finch asked.

"Hostage situation," Russo said shortly, and disappeared into the crowd. They could see that the large window of the president's office facing the quad had been shattered. As they made their way closer to Woodfin, they saw a tight group of people around a man lying on the grass.

"What happened?" Finch asked a student.

"Dr. Dobbs," the boy said, "he got shot in the ass."

"Couldn't happen to a nicer person," Willow said.

Inside the president's office the phone rang. Cowan motioned with his gun to Big Hoss. "Answer it," he said, "Tell them everything I want."

"Shit," Big Hoss said, "give me the list." Eloise handed him the pad. He picked up the phone. "Hello?" he said. Then, "Yes, this is the fucking president's office! How can I help you?" He listened for a while, nodding his head from time to time. "All right," he said. He sat holding the phone. "They say, first of all, for you to give yourself up, Cowan, make it easy on yourself. If you won't do that, then you should release your hostages, starting with the women. Then all of us. One at a time." He looked around the room. The noise from outside sounded like a football game. "But what the hell," he said, "I wouldn't mind you starting with old shitty pants over there."

"You are fired!" Stegall said, "clean out your office!"

"Shut up! Both of you!" Cowan said. "Read them the list of demands. Tell them I ain't releasing anybody till we get to Cuba. Tell them I've got a bomb in this satchel that will blow us all to kingdom come! And add to the list: I want a limo big enough to hold us all to take us out to the strip."

"A bomb!?" Alberta exclaimed. She started to wail again.

"What fucking strip?" Hoss asked and snorted. Cowan aimed the gun right at Hoss's head. "Okay, okay," Hoss said. He began to read the demands into the phone. "Yeah, yeah, that's what I said," he said. He read the rest of the demands. Then he laughed, as though the person on the other end had made a joke. He listened again for a few minutes. "He says he has a bomb. Blamo!" Hoss said. After a few seconds, he held the phone out. "They want to talk to you," he said.

"Tell them to go fuck themselves and get busy with the jet and all."

"I'll relay the message," Hoss said, and repeated what Cowan had said. He listened, nodding from time to time. "They want to know," he said, "if you're talking about the old Wilmer Flowers strip between here and Crestview."

"Tell them hell yeah!"

"They say that strip ain't long enough for a jet," Hoss said.

"Tell them bullshit! It was long enough for Wilmer's jet when he was flying in dope from South America. I know. I distributed for him. I went on a couple of trips with him. Tell them they're full of crap! Tell them all of that. Tell them I cried when I read in the papers that they'd busted old Wilmer, who was a better man than all of them put together! Tell them all of that!"

"Okay, okay," Hoss said. He repeated everything as accurately as he could. When he was finished, Hoss said to Cowan, "They said, 'fuck you.'" They hadn't, but Hoss felt they should have. In Hoss's opinion, they were being entirely too coddling of this psycho.

Cowan laughed. "They meant fuck *you,* shit-for-brains," he said.

They waited. All four of the hostages' legs had gotten cramped and tired. Their legs were trembling. The stench in the room had not abated much, even with the wide open window. Long minutes went by, as they listened to the noise from the quad.

"They're probably selling T shirts and beer," Hoss said. He and Cowan laughed jovially and the others looked horrified. An hour went by. Another. They had pretty much lost all sense of time, not trusting their watches, which seemed not to move at all.

There was a sudden clanking on the floor and they all stared at a hissing canister that had come through the window. "Tear Gas!" Cowan exclaimed. He grabbed the bomb and threw it back out the window, where it exploded on contact with one of the police cars. They could all see the white cloud of gas that wafted out over the throng, into the live oaks, on the southerly breeze. There was howling and wailing as the gas hit the crowd. After a minute, the phone rang again, and Big Hoss answered it.

"Shit, man, you were going to gas us all!" he said. He listened for a minute or two. "Okay, okay," he said, "yeah, yeah. All right, I hear you. Better to be gassed than dead. Okay. Well, fuck it. Isn't there some other course of action you motherfuckers could take? Come on! Somewhere between getting gassed and dead! Come on, earn your pay!"

"Don't talk to the police like that," Eloise Hoyle said. "They are our only hope."

Hoss shrugged. He still had the phone to his ear and he waved for her to be quiet. After a minute or two he said, "No shit?! Jesus F. Christ!" He covered the phone. "They say they've got your limo ready. And the jet's on the strip, ready to go. I think they've lost their fucking minds."

"Line up," Cowan said, "one behind the other. Hug the one in front of you. Shit-for-brains, you get behind Stegall."

"Aww, hell," Hoss whined, "not that, whew! They're lying to you, Cowan. There ain't no jet."

"There better be," Cowan said. He reached into the satchel and pulled out a forty-five automatic and a hand grenade. "This forty-five goes in your back, Hoss, and this grenade next to your and the president's neck. And see this?" There was a cord attached to the pin on the grenade. Cowan pulled it tight and put the other end in his teeth. "You folks remember: any funny business, from *any-body*, and I pull the trigger. This fucker will go through all four of you!" Alberta whimpered. "And I yank the grenade with my teeth. Smithereens! Goodbye everybody!" Both women were crying now. Cowan strapped the satchel to his back. He looked out the window. "There it is," he said. "Long and black and shiny. Just like I ordered. Us folks are traveling in style."

"You'll never get away with this, Cowan," Hoss said.

"Watch me," Cowan said. "Now hug up. Start marching to the door." They stumbled over each other's legs. "Careful! No funny business. Walk in step. All right, that's better." They moved clumsily through the outer office and into the foyer; the front door was propped open and the sun was brilliant and intense on the carpet. They could all see the waiting limo outside, the morning sun glistening on its polish. They got to the door and began to move outside. "Any false move and they're all dead!" Cowan shouted. The policemen were showing their empty hands over their heads.

"What's wrong with those dumb-ass motherfuckers?" Hoss barked.

"They're trying to keep us from getting killed, *Dean* Murphy, so just shut up," John Stegall said.

They went down the sidewalk to the waiting limousine. One by one they got in. The crowd looked on in tense silence. The limo started; the windows were tinted, and no one could see inside. It glided down the brick street and through the gate and turned left on Juniper Street. The policemen jumped into their cars and prepared to follow, as did the SWAT tank.

Lily, Finch and Willow stood staring at the developments. They watched the parade of squad cars move off the campus. People then began to chatter and stir. "Where are they going?" they heard one student ask. Another answered, "I heard a policeman say they're headed out to the old air strip. They're flying to Cuba!" "Cuba?" "Yeah, Cuba!"

"Cuba!?" Willow said to the other two. "Why would he want to go to Cuba?"

"Out of the country, I guess," Finch said. "Cowan doesn't know anything. He's ignorant, and stupid."

"Yeah, and dangerous. But not to us, I guess. He's gone," Lily said.

"For the moment, anyway," Willow said. "Those four looked terrified. I thought poor Alberta was going to faint. What was that he was holding in his left hand against the president's neck?"

"Someone said it was a hand grenade," Finch said. "And he has a bomb in that backpack, I heard."

All of a sudden the students began to sprint away from the quad. Finch grabbed one by the arm. "What's going on?"

"Everybody's getting their cars. We're all going out there!" he said.

They looked at each other. "Well, hell," Finch said, "let's go get my car and go, too!"

Willow sniffed at Finch's car. "Not a word!" Finch cautioned her, "get your ass in!"

Lily got into the back seat, shoveling aside old fast food wrappers and empty liquor bottles. Willow rode shotgun, and Finch drove through the campus. He pulled into the line of cars headed out of town.

"This is absurd," Willow said.

"Yeah, isn't it?" Finch said, and they all three roared with delight. It was exhilarating, and the irony of their cheerfulness caused them to laugh even harder. Their hilarity spilled out of the open windows and caught the attention of people standing on the sidewalks when they went through downtown. They passed Stache's and there was a crowd out front cheering and applauding the parade of cars.

"I'm surprised you didn't stop by your office," Willow said when her giggling subsided.

"No need," Finch said. He reached under the seat and pulled out a bottle of Laproaig, which he passed over the seat to Lily in the back. "Lily, girl," he said, "find some paper cups or something and fix us all a drink!"

Lily fished around in the detritus in the back seat and found a tube of plastic cups. She cut the seal on the Laproaig with her fingernail, pulled out the stopper, poured them each a couple of fingers and passed theirs back up front.

"Good girl!" Finch said.

"I'm not used to drinking it this way," Willow said.

"Just sip it, dear Willow," Finch said. "It's full of the smoke from the peat fires of Scotland!"

"Oh, my, it's delicious," Willow said.

The parade continued out of town and down a two lane road through twisted live oaks and palmettos. There were mobile homes and small cottages along the way, and people were standing in the sandy front yards shouting encouragement as they went by. They heard the chopping of a helicopter overhead. "They must be covering this on the television," Finch said. Sure enough, as the helicopter moved ahead of them, they could read the letters WTSB-TV on the side. "That's a Tallahassee station," Finch said.

"Yes," Willow said, "the one with the cheerful coffee drinkers in the morning. Dreadful people."

As they approached the air strip they could see blue lights flashing up ahead. Cars were peeling off to the sides of the road, but Finch kept going. Students and some faculty were sprinting along the roadside. They saw Garcia Russo scurry by, followed by R. D. Wettermark. "I guess their buddy Dobbs is still back there with a tourniquet on his fat ass," Finch said, and they all convulsed, howling. They were giddy. The atmosphere was carnival-like, people swirling ahead, the police trying to disperse them. The helicopter hovered overhead, kicking up clouds of sand, and they could see a sleek jet airplane sitting on the runway. A policeman frantically waved Finch down and he ground to a halt. Through the shimmering heat waves rising from the pavement of the strip they could see the limousine sitting next to the airplane.

"Where the hell you think you're going?" the policeman grunted at Finch.

"That's my president in there," Finch said, "I want to save him. I want to take his place!" They all burst out laughing. The policeman looked quizzically at them.

"This ain't no joke!" he barked. "Now get this heap of junk out of the middle of the road!" He was leaning in the driver's side window. He sniffed. "Y'all been drinking!" he said, "just park it right over there, I'll get to y'all after a while."

Finch backed up. There were yells of "Hey!" and "Motherfucker!" from the people in the road. Finch made a U turn and parked headed away from the airstrip. Some students pounded on the hood of his car. One of them said, surprised, "Oh, hey, Mr. Finch. Hey, Dr. Behn." They didn't respond.

"Something, ain't it?" the student said.

"Yes," Willow said. "Something, indeed."

They got out of the car. The crowd of onlookers was now pushing against the yellow police tape cordoning off the runway. They saw the hostages, still clutched together, awkwardly mounting the stairs of the plane, with Rudolph Cowan behind them. The police were yelling at the gathering to stay back. They watched as the door to the plane closed and the limo pulled away. The jet taxied to the end of the runway, turned around, and sped down the runway. It lifted into the air. A huge cheer went up from the crowd as the plane continued upward. They were all as heedlessly bemused as Finch, Willow and Lily. The idea of little President John W. Stegall and Big Hoss Murphy flying off to Cuba with Rudolph Cowan was too engagingly comical. They had forgotten about Alberta and Eloise, about the grave seriousness of the situation. Gradually the commotion began to die down, as perhaps they began to remember those things. A great quiet settled over the gathered throng.

They all watched the plane as it rose higher and higher into the air, the sun reflecting off its wings. It got smaller and smaller, until it was just a shiny speck against the high cerulean sky, sparkling like an early star.

CHAPTER SIXTEEN

Two months later, all five of them, Cowan, Big Hoss, Alberta, Eloise and John Stegall, along with the pilot, were still in a Cuban jail. None of them had any travel documents, and in Cuba it would not have mattered if they *had* had them. There was much speculation about why the Cuban authorities allowed them to land in the first place. Fidel Castro was seen on state television denouncing them as spies, which generated considerable amusement on the Lakewood campus. The campus had been abuzz with it all in the weeks leading up to finals and graduation. There was general agreement that the police, and the FBI, which had been called in, had made a monumental mess of handling the hostage situation. Everyone had an opinion. The Federal government remained "cautiously optimistic" but claimed they could not comment further because of the delicacy of the diplomatic situation in Cuba.

Garcia Russo exclaimed: "They should have wiped those bastards out at the Bay of Pigs! How dare they put godless communism in my homeland!?"

"Your homeland?" R. D. Wettermark said. "I thought you were born in Meridian, Mississippi."

"I was!" Russo huffed, "to Cuban ancestors!"

Willow thought it was a total and complete disaster. "They should have put that Cowan back in jail as soon as he got out," she said. "They should never let a man like that run loose among civilized people."

"That's not how it works, Willow," Lily said.

"Well, it *should* work that way," Willow said.

Dean Wallace Jefferson was devastated and enraged when the Board of Trust put Lillian Lallo in as interim president. He got exceedingly drunk and stomped around their cramped house throwing things. He threw hairbrushes and mirrors, coffee cups and plates. He was furious; he seethed morosely and then erupted into more hurling. Paulette threatened to cut off his liquor supply; he threatened to kill her if she did. She left the house and went over to Rufus Doublet's apartment, where she moved in. They planned to get married when Paulette divorced her obese maniac of a husband. Paulette was thirteen years older than Doublet, but that suited him just fine.

Shortly after Paulette left him, Dean Jefferson sent a barely legible, handwritten letter to the Board of Trust resigning his position and offering a sinister, bullying warning, bordering on terrorizing, that he would exact his revenge on them for going back on their word and would sue the school "for every penny in its fucking coffers." He then drove away from Lakewood in his Buick, and no one had heard from him, nor seen him, since.

The Board appointed Dr. Fred C. Dobbs interim dean, since he had, in their words, "been wounded in the faithful and responsible committal of his duties and should be justly rewarded."

"From one fat slob to another," was Brasfield Finch's comment.

It was all too much for Lily. She was mystified and appalled by the whole episode and everything that followed. She was flabbergasted. "Has this school totally lost its mind?" she asked Willow in frustration.

"Whatever small mind it ever had, yes!" Willow replied.

"What will become of us? Lillian Lallo? *Fred C. Dobbs*? My God!"

"Who else was the Board going to appoint as president, that dreadful Wallace Jefferson? Good riddance to him!"

"With Dobbs in as dean," Lily said, "the English department's goose is cooked. It'll be all science now. All Harmon Hall. At least Jefferson was a humanities man."

"I'm afraid you're right, Lily dear," said Willow. "Though to call that awful man a humanities man is a stretch."

Two days after Lillian Lallo began warming the office chair

in the president's office, Brasfield Finch received a memo from her informing him that his MFA was no longer sufficient to maintain his position. It was recommended that he return to graduate school and work on a doctorate. Otherwise he would be reduced to the rank of instructor and would no longer be eligible to teach his writing workshops, which were junior-senior level.

"Who the hell is going to teach them?" Finch asked Lily. "What do they think they're doing?!"

"They'll probably not be offered," Lily said, "Dobbs will see to that."

"Fuck it!" Finch said. "After my thirty years here and then this. Fuck it!"

Who, indeed, would teach the workshops? Katharine Klinger and Eleanor Buffkin had announced their retirements, commencing after graduation that academic year. That meant there would be two tenure level slots to be filled, and Rufus Doublet would possibly search for a writer who held a PHD. But that was unlikely; the two positions would almost certainly be filled with "scholars."

One day during finals, Dr. Dobbs called Lily over to his office, an enclave that still smelled of Jefferson's flabby body; the odor was perhaps magnified by the presence of yet another fleshy torso.

"Well, Lily," Dobbs said, licking his liver lips. His blue tie was askew and his collar was curled up around his chin. He immediately focused on her legs in her mini skirt. He spoke directly to her crotch. "I suppose now the door is open. You can take over all of old Buffkin's courses."

"I'm confused, Dr. Dobbs," Lily said.

"Confused? What do you mean confused? I'm doing you a favor, Lily. I'm looking out for you. You want the American lit courses, don't you? I can make that happen."

"This is all too much for me," she said.

"What? Oh, you mean my wound. Well, it's healing nicely.

Would you like to see?" He grinned slyly at her.

"No, no, I didn't mean your wound. I mean just...just everything."

"You're sure you don't want to look at it?" he said. "My wife tells me I have a fine ass."

She just stared at him. After a few moments she said, "I'm sure it is, Dr. Dobbs, but it is of no interest to me."

"Oh, come on, now, girl. I'm taking care of you, I want you to take care of me." She didn't respond. "Pretty girls know how to take care of a man. Don't *you*?"

She rose from the chair. "Dr. Dobbs, I have a final to give," she said, "so if you'll excuse me I'll just be going."

"Remember this conversation, girl," he said to her back. She stopped at the door and turned around to face him.

"I'm not a 'girl,'" she said, "and, believe me, I *will* remember it."

Lily found herself immersed in the worst depression she had ever experienced. All the events of the recent weeks seemed to her to totally, finally, negate all the excitement and idealism she had initially brought to her career as a college teacher. Her world was as flat as an undercooked pancake. She could think of only one thing she had really enjoyed and found gratification from during her second year of teaching, and that had been the play she was in. There were her friendships/relationships with Brass and Willow, of course. She felt sure they would remain close for life. But she had made no other real friends; that, certainly, was her own fault, but it was true nonetheless. She could not bear the thought of another dreary year at Lakewood. Admittedly, there had been excitement—the play, the chaos of the hostage circumstances that had both amused her and frightened her and left her weak—but weeks of paper grading and new preparations had worn her down. Her students didn't seem as lively as they had the first year, which she was quick to concede was probably all her fault as well. She just didn't seem to have the energy she had had the first year.

Her sexual affair with Charlie Stewart had left her drained. Since he had departed Lakewood, Lily had had no cravings to sleep with a man at all. She still had spent the night at Willow's apartment from time to time; the older woman's sex drive was not nearly as strong as Lily's, but Lily found a lot of comfort in their nearness. All in all, she was just down.

On a soft, early summer evening, as the sun eased slowly down in the western sky, Willow, Brass and Lily sat around a table on the porch at Stache's. It was not yet hot enough to drive people inside and the three of them were enjoying the mellow breezes—smelling of salt and sunlight—that came all the way from the Gulf. It was two days after graduation; the academic year was sealed up and put away.

After Randy served them their drinks—gin and tonic for the two women, Scotch on the rocks for Finch—they relaxed in their rickety chairs and took the first few sips. They all chuckled when Finch pointed out that someone had scratched "Fuck Stegall" on the scarred tabletop. Finch sighed deeply and said,

"Whew. What a year!"

"Wasn't it though?" Willow replied.

They sat without speaking for a few minutes, listening to the chatter from the other end of the porch, a long table with a bunch of men from the maintenance department who gathered every late afternoon to drink beer. They were always there, in their green uniforms, drinking Pabst Blue Ribbon, pouring it from the cans.

"I hope they're getting ready to do their summer maintenance work in the classroom buildings," Willow said. "There's a wasp nest up in the ceiling somewhere over my office, and every now and then one swoops down as if it's going to attack me, then it buzzes around on the ceiling, bumping against the windows. It's frightening. I usually kill them with a fat edition of *The Southern Review* that I keep on my desk."

"Ugh," Lily said, "I think I would vacate my office!"

"Way to go, Willow," Finch said, "the great white huntress!"

"Mr. Finch," Willow said, chortling, "you manage to be both racist and sexist in one sentence!" They all cackled; they felt good in the late sunshine. The summer stretched before them. It was going to be a sublime Florida sunset.

"Are you going back to London, Willow?" Lily asked.

"No," she replied, "I've finished all the research. I'm going to attempt to grind out a first draft of my book. Though I must admit, I'm growing somewhat weary of Sand. I suppose familiarity breeds…well, certainly not contempt."

"Boredom?" Finch asked.

"Perhaps you could say that," Willow said. "It's more that I just don't seem to have the same enthusiasm or energy I had in the beginning."

"Understandable," Finch said. "How about you, Lily?"

Lily hesitated. "I don't know," she finally said. "All three of us know that I haven't written word one on my dissertation since I've been here. I also recognize that I seem to have lost my burning interest in Toni Morrison, though I still think she's a great writer. I don't know. It just seems like drudgery now. Writing about her work."

"You don't need to be a critic, Lily," Finch said. He frowned when he said the word *critic*. "What you are, what you were born to be, is an actor!"

"On, now, don't start that," Lily said.

"Tell me, sweetheart, when were you the happiest and most content during this past year?" Finch asked.

"The play, of course," Lily said. "But…"

"You were sensational in *A Doll's House*, Lily," Willow said, "you were spectacular!"

"Come on," Lily said, "it was just a college theater production." She was shaking her head no. She wanted them to change the subject. "Let's talk about Brass. I mean, what a terrible blow, man!"

Finch waved his hands in the air, dismissing her attempt to alter the conversation. "Oh no you don't! Wait a minute! Yes, the production was 'college,' but *your* performance was pro! You are a natural, Lily, no two ways about it."

"Well..." she said. She thought for a minute. "In the remote event that you are right, what the hell do I do about it? Audition for another J. J. Underwood epic?"

"No!" Finch said. "You must go to New York!"

"New York?! Brass, you can't be serious."

"As serious as an oil spill!" Finch said. Randy appeared at the table, having seen Finch's gesture with his hands. He had a new buzz cut. "What happened to your pony tail?!" Finch asked, aghast.

"Cut it off," Randy said, "another round?" They all nodded yes.

"But you had it when you waited on us ten minutes ago!" Finch said.

"Lulu just cut it for me," he said, "shaved my head." He walked back to the bar, wiping his hands on his apron.

"Poor boy," Finch said, "he just lost the only distinguishing characteristic he ever had."

"It'll grow back," Willow said.

"Let's get off this New York nonsense," Lily said. "Brass, what in the world are you going to do about your position and all?"

"Well," he said, sipping his fresh drink. "I've been giving it a lot of thought. I'm certainly not going to slide back and be an instructor; I couldn't bear talking to those vacant-faced freshmen and sophomores. It would be humiliating, which is what the administration intends, I'm sure. And at my age, I'm not going back to school to work on any doctorate; I've been around long enough to know that most people with doctorates—I said *most* people, Willow—just stayed in school too long. Present company certainly excluded, of course." He smiled at them. "So what will I do? Well, I want to finish my novel, for one thing. And I don't have to stay around here to do it."

"You're thinking of *leaving*? Oh, no!" Lily said. She looked as though she were about to cry.

"Hear me out," Brass said. "Lily, have you signed your contract for next year yet?"

"No, I just got it," Lily said. "With a hefty five thousand dollar raise. There was a note scribbled at the bottom. 'From your very good friend, who takes care of you, Fred C. Dobbs, Dean of the College, PHD.' He even drew a little heart. I almost puked."

"Well, okay," Finch said, settling back, "here's my proposition. I've got a good bit of money saved up, mainly because I just don't ever really think of spending any of it. As you know, my wardrobe budget is not large." They all laughed. "And I hardly drive a luxury car." (More chuckling.) "Anyway, if I'm to lose my hard earned high paying position as Associate Professor," (A smile.) "then I better be thinking of something else. I feel sure that once they establish me as an instructor, they'll take away my tenure, too, and I would be out on my ass."

"Can they do that?!" Lily exclaimed.

"My dear," Finch said, "administrators can do anything they want to do, short of getting themselves out of Cuban jails." He sniggered sardonically. "So what I propose is this: we both, Lily, resign our positions here, such as they are, and move to New York."

"But…" Lily began.

"Just…just hear me out, okay? I have more than enough money to keep us going for a year, I think. We can get us a small furnished apartment and set up housekeeping. I can work on my novel, perhaps finish it, and you could take acting lessons or go to auditions or whatever it is that aspiring actors do in New York. I've thought this through. I can put my furniture in storage and sell my car. Anything you want to store, Lily, like that new couch and your bed could go in with my stuff. Now you just send that contract back unsigned and let's get the fucking hell out of here!"

Lily sat very still, looking from one of them to the other. She chewed on her lip. She looked pleadingly at Willow, and Willow nodded yes. *I don't know! I don't know!* Then, without warning and so swiftly that it made her head jerk back Lily felt an overwhelming sense of freedom, glorious freedom. She said quickly, before the moment passed,

"Okay!"

Both Willow and Brass smiled warmly at her.

"Okay," she said, again, more softly.

THE END

William Cobb held a Fellowship in Fiction Writing from the National Endowment for the Arts (1979), received grants in both drama and Fiction from the Alabama State Council on the Arts in 1989 and 1994, and was a Fellow in Playwriting at the Atlantic Center for the Arts in New Smyrna Beach, Florida, in 1985. A native of Demopolis, Alabama, he attended Livingston State College, now The University of West Alabama, where he was named Distinguished Alumnus of the Year, and Vanderbilt University. He was a member of The Authors Guild and his biography appears in CONTEMPORARY NOVELISTS. He was for twelve years Writer-in-Residence at The University of Montevallo in Alabama.

In addition to his fiction, Cobb wrote for the stage. Three of his plays, SUNDAY'S CHILD, A PLACE OF SPRINGS, and EARLY RAINS were produced Off-Broadway in New York, and SUNDAY'S CHILD, which starred noted Academy Award-winning actress Celeste Holm in the New York production, was seen in two regional productions. A newly revised version of SUNDAY'S CHILD was given a staged reading at Southern Playworks in Birmingham. At the time of his death, William was planning to take Lily and Brass to NYC, entering them both in the world of theater there and this completing this trilogy.